Thus Spoke the Bible:

Basics of Biblical Narratives

Thus Spoke the Bible:

Basics of Biblical Narratives

Antony John Baptist

2016

Thus Spoke the Bible: Basics of Biblical Narratives – published by the Rev. Dr. Ashish Amos of the Indian Society for Promoting Christian Knowledge (ISPCK), Post Box 1585, Kashmere Gate, Delhi-110006.

© Author, 2016

ISBN: 978-84-8465-565-0

Laser typeset by

ISPCK, Post Box 1585, 1654, Madarsa Road, Kashmere Gate, Delhi-110006 • *Tel:* 23866323

e-mail: ashish@ispck.org.in • ella@ispck.org.in
website: www.ispck.org.in

Dedicated
To Most Rev. Dr. J. Susaimanickam,
Chairman of TNBC and CCBI Commissions for Bible
on his 70th Birthday

To Frau Rosi Pabst, Germany,
on her 80th Birthday.

Contents

Foreword - 1

"God speaks in Sacred Scriptures through men in human fashion," recalled the Dogmatic Constitution *Dei Verbum* on Divine Revelation of Vatican II (no. 12). For a long time and probably under the influence of Hegelianism, this "human fashion" was understood in terms of historical criticism: Biblical interpretation consisted in retracing the history of the formation of the text from tradition to written sources and the progressive constitution of larger and larger units until the present text came into existence. An example of the application of this method can be found in the Vatican Document itself outlining the three stages of Gospel formation in its chapter on the New Testament (*Dei Verbum* no. 19). The limitations of this method were clearly exposed by Karl Barth in the Introduction of his commentary on *Romans*. Historical criticism dismantles the text rather than leading to real understanding and is therefore pastorally ineffective.

Now Scripture studies have taken a new turn. A new methodology has shifted from the Scriptures as the outcome of a historical development to the Scriptures as literature, from the genetic perspective to the actual impact of the text. In technical terms exegesis is invited to move from the diachronic to the synchronic approach. In plain terms, the new approach consists in taking the Scriptures just as writings, literary products, works of art, whether it be scribal or popular art.

Since a good part of the Bible is made of narrations, narrative analysis is one of the main forms of this study of the "Bible as Literature." The approach has rapidly developed into a well analysed technique. We are grateful to Antony John Baptist for giving us a competent and lucid presentation of this new method. He does not reject historical criticism but emphasizes the consideration of the text in its "wholeness." As he puts it in the introductory chapter, "both historical study and artistic study are important. While Historical Critical Method helps in historical study, Narrative Criticism takes us to the artistic study of the Bible... Narrative Criticism does not deny the fact that the text has undergone such a *history/ tradition.*" And he quotes Kenneth R. R. Gros Louis, "A literary interpretation of the Bible in no way replaces or invalidates other approaches- source analysis, anthropology, sociology, theology, archaeology, comparative religion- nor does it seek to rival in authority the centuries of interpretations in commentaries." Yet "Narrative Criticism takes the final stage of the text seriously and studies it as a literature. This way of doing is more viable and the results are more reliable."

Adopting a new technology is no easy task and, in its newly developed technical form, new narratology could appear as complex as historical criticism of old. But Antony John Baptist illustrates his exposition with enlightening references to the use he made of the method in his doctoral thesis on Hagar story in Gen 16 (*Together as Sisters: Hagar and Dalit Women,* New Delhi: ISPCK, 2012).

The reference of the Dissertation to Dalit theology is significant. In his often repeated criticism of the historico-critical method, the regretted George Soares Prabhu, the pioneer of inculturated biblical studies in India, called for "an exegetical model for India" that would be relevant to the struggles of the masses. The manual of narratology presented by Antony John Baptist and its application to the Dalit problem in his thesis respond to the need expressed by Soares Prabhu. They show that narratology can open the way to socio-economic relevant exegesis.

Soares Prabhu advocated also a rhetorical poetics that would be "enriched by contributions from the as yet largely untapped but fantastically rich fields of Indian linguistics and poetics" in the *dhavani* theory for instance (*Biblical Themes for Contextual Theology Today*, Pune, 1999, p 217). This would open still another line of research. A wide field opens itself to Indian Exegesis and Hermeneutics. Antony John Baptist's contribution is a valuable step on newly opened ways.

L. Legrand
Professor of the New Testament
St. Peter's Pontifical Institute
Bangalore, India.

Foreword - 2

This is the first introduction to Biblical narratology written by an Indian theologian and expert of Biblical studies. Its very clear structure and plain language makes it easy to read. The author uses a wide variety of classics in the field of narratological approaches to the Bible to create a new manual for students or readers interested in Biblical story telling. Readers will find succinct explanations of technical terms and lots of illustrating examples taken from biblical narratives. At the same time, the author takes great care to show how narratology contributes to reading the Bible as Scripture for a community of believers. An indispensable tool of biblical studies!

Prof. Dr. Marie-Theres Wacker
Professor of Old Testament
Faculty of Catholic Theology,
University of Muenster/Germany,
Member of the board of directors of "Concilium"

Preface

The days of my stay at Rome for four years for the study of Bible were of happy memories. The classes of Prof. Jean – Louis Ska introduced me the world of Narrative Criticism. Back in the country I applied this field of study to my doctoral research on Hagar episode in Gen 16. This is the off shoot of these two intellectual endeavors in my life. When I did my doctoral studies I kept accumulating the theories and examples of Narrative Criticism. Last summer I had the chance to stay with Frau Rosi Pabst for a month. There the accumulated notes took the present shape of a book. I thank her profusely for her love, hospitality and the atmosphere she created in her house for an intellectual activity. I also wish her *Ad multos Annos* as she celebrates her 80th birthday.

Prof. L. Legrand is a pioneer in Biblical Studies in India. He has always encouraged and supported my publications and biblical activities. He has forwarded my book as 'a valuable step on newly opened ways'. I sincerely thank him. Prof. Dr. Marie – Theres Wacker, Professor of Old Testament, University of Muenster, Germany, had not only given a forward to my book but also read the whole manuscript and given me necessary corrections and points for improving it. I thank for the third, they were only happen to publish this too. I thank Rev. Dr. Ashish Amos, and all the staff associated with the publication of this book especially Ms. Ella Sonawane.

My bishop Most Rev. Dr. P. Soundararaju, sdb, Bishop of Vellore, is delighted whenever I bring out a new book. I thank him for his encouragement and support. My chairman bishop, Most Rev. Dr. J. Susaimanickam, Bishop of Sivagangai, is a source of inspiration to me. His constant contribution in Biblical field for the church of Tamilnadu and India is a model for my ministry in the regional commission for Bible. I wish and pray for God's blessings on him as he completes his 70th birthday.

My priest friends Rev. Fr. Vinoth and Rev. Fr. Arockia Raj OFM Cap always support my publications. Together with them there is a network of friends who always encourage and support me. I thank them all and the present TNBCLC community at Tindivanam.

I only wish and pray that this book on Narrative Criticism helps the Indian students of Scripture to take their biblical studies seriously and go as deep as possible to bring out the great treasures hidden in the Holy Scriptures.

In the ministry of God's Word,

Dr. Antony John Baptist

Abbreviations

AnBib	AnalectaBiblica
AOAT	Alter Orient und Altes Testament
Bib	Biblica
BiRes	Biblical Research
BR	Bible Review
CBQ	The Catholic Biblical Quarterly
JSNT	Journal for the Study of the New Testament
JSOT	Journal for the Study of the Old Testament
JSOTSS	Journal for the Study of the Old Testament Supplement Series
SubBib	Subsidia Biblica
VT	Vetus Testamentum
VTS	Supplements to Vetus Testamentum
ZAW	Zeitschrift für die Alttestamentliche Wissenschaft

Introduction

In India, the interest for Biblical Studies is picking up gradually in all the churches. Students, scholars, priests and pastors and a considerable number of Laity are dedicating their time and energy to search and interpret the Scriptures. The manuals of scriptural studies are very limited in India. Most of the time, we have to depend on the West for the tools of exegesis. Since English is not our native tongue we are not able to benefit much from these foreign manuals. So I thought it is the need of the time to produce some manuals in India itself, of course, borrowing the rich contributions of the scholars of the West. So I have attempted this book on Narrative Criticism mainly for the Indian Students of Sacred Scriptures. The style of English is very simple and direct. I have kept the technical terms to the minimum. If I had to use them I have tried to give some simple explanations to them with some examples from the Bible.

At Pontifical Biblical Institute, Rome, I did some courses, which used Narrative Criticism. When I did my doctoral studies in the Department of Christian Studies, University of Madras, I had the chance to devote more time to study some books on Narrative Criticism. I have applied all that I studied on this criticism to my text (Gen 16- The Hagar Episode). This was published under the title, *Together as Sisters: Hagar and Dalit Women*, by ISPCK, Delhi. All that is explained in this book is applied to Gen 16. So the students have a standing example of how to apply the theories and manuals to a particular text. Therefore this book is a blend of theory and application to a text. And where possible and needed I have given also scriptural references where the particular idea can be applied or seen.

Purposely, I have kept the linguistic requirement to the minimum. Because most of the seekers of the 'Word of God' in India are not well-versed in Biblical languages. So ignorance of Hebrew or Greek should in no way hinder or deter one to read this book or to do exegetical study. However I do not deny the fact that, the knowledge of Biblical Languages will help all the more in doing exegesis.

Though I have heavily quoted various authors, I have kept the bibliography and the difference of opinions among them to the footnotes. The main purpose of the book is to explain the concepts and the tools of study relating to Narrative Criticism and not to discuss the difference of opinions between the authors. In short, this book aims to bring together the ideas of the leading authors of Narrative Criticism in one book or manual, to explain them in simple terms with examples and apply them to Gen 16.

I, in no way, claim that this book is the exhaustive one on the subject. I am aware that I have not covered all the areas of Narrative Criticism. Moreover I have depended only on those books I could collect during my doctoral studies. I admit that there are more literature available on the topic than that are cited here.

If this book helps the students of Sacred Scripture to understand it and make sense of the narrative part of the Bible, I think, this book has reached its purpose.

CHAPTER - 1

Some Preliminary Considerations: Narratology or Narrative Criticism

The Need

The major part of the Bible, both Old Testament and the New Testament consists of narration. The whole of Historical Books (Genesis to Nehemiah) and 1-2 Maccabees[1] in the Old Testament and the Gospels and the Acts in the New Testament fall in this category. One can roughly say that one third of the Old Testament and more than a half of the New Testament consist of narration. As early as Martin Luther, scholars were aware of the use of Narrative criticism. Paul R. House quotes Martin Luther, "certainly it is my desire that there shall be as many poets and rhetoricians as possible, because I see that by these studies, as by no other means, people are wonderfully fitted for the grasping of sacred truth and for handing it skilfully and happily".[2] Paul R. House further says, "the great reformer acknowledged the need to grasp the Bible's literary components".[3] So it is important to know how to understand the narration in the Bible.

By now we know that the narration in the Bible is not like 'reporting or documentation' of today's world. It is something more than that. It wants to communicate an idea or ideology, in the religious circle, we may call it theology, that is truths about God, His interaction in the human history and the future of human destiny etc. So it is important to know not only to read the Biblical texts but also to understand them rightly and come to right understanding of it, namely what is the idea or ideology or theology it wants to communicate. The reading of the text and making sense of it has its own rules and techniques, which is called narratology or narrative criticism. This book tries to introduce it systematically and as simply as possible.

Definition of Narrative Criticism

D.F. Tolmie defines Narrative Criticism as "the systematic study of the typical features of narrative texts"[4]. It studies "the way the narrative components work to create a story".[5] M.C. de Boer would say, "Narrative criticism explores the ways in which an implied author determines an implied reader's response (through the medium of the text)".[6]

Questions Studied

Kenneth R.R. Gros Louis[7] gives a long list of questions that are to be asked when studying a text according to narrative criticism, such as structure, subject of narrative, characters, dialogues, actions, and reader. M. Sternberg would add some more to it such as plot, characterization, point of view, setting, symbolism, irony, themes, motifs, informational gap, redundancy, allusion, metaphor, modes of speech etc.[8] Here the focus is not only what the text says but also *how* it says what it wants to say. Putting together all the subject matters of Narrative Criticism we can say that narrative criticism studies *what and why* (structure and plot), *the who* (characters), the *when and where* (setting), and the *wherefore* (point of view) of the narration/ text.

Merits and Defects of Using Narrative Criticism

As any system of Biblical Criticism, Narrative Criticism, too, has its merits and difficulties. It is useful to be aware of them before venturing into a detailed study of Narrative Criticism and its techniques.

According to R. Alter it is "pleasurable rather than arduous".[9] Quoting Gunkel, Bar-Efrat says that, "anyone who did not pay attention to their artistic form was not only deprived of considerable pleasure but also failed to clarify their meaning".[10] Bar-Efrat further argues that "it is impossible to appreciate the nature of biblical narrative fully, understand the network of its component elements or penetrate into its inner world without having recourse to the methods and tools of literary scholarship".[11] Bible is also a literary work. So Adele Berlin says, "literary works should be analysed according to the principles of literary science".[12] So we need to use literary criticism like narrative criticism to understand the message and to appreciate the richness of the Bible.[13] Alter is right when he says, "As one discovers how to adjust the fine focus of those literary binoculars, the biblical tales, forceful enough to begin with, show a surprising subtlety and inventiveness of detail, and in many instances a beautifully interwoven wholeness."[14] Against the claim that historical criticism can reveal the author's intention, Paul R. House argues that, "language and style may reveal as much about an author's intentions as that author's historical situation".[15] He is convinced that "Intention and meaning will emerge as a thorough examination of linguistic patterns and artistic texture takes place".[16] So it is very clear that Narrative Criticism helps to bring out the inner meaning/s of the text.

Now, regarding *difficulties* in using Narrative criticism, most of the times the authors of narrative criticism tend to use the biblical passage "as though it were a unitary production just like a modern novel that is entirely conceived and executed by a single independent writer who supervises his original work from first draft to page proofs."[17] So we cannot undermine the contribution of historical critical method about formation of the text or a book of Bible. David M. Gunn points out the challenges one has to face when he/she uses narrative criticism and says, "... reading biblical narrative in terms of its final form really is a more radical proposition than perhaps is realized by those who most enthusiastically have embraced the program...Are the books of Samuel a book or not? Is this work a narrative? What about Deuteronomy to 2 Kings? Or the whole Hebrew canon? In each case, is the question whether we have "a" narrator, let alone a reliable one, real?"[18]

Obviously, Narrative criticism can be applied only to those narrative parts of the Bible and it cannot be applied to all the sections of the bible. For example, texts such as Laws, Poems, Prophetic and Wisdom Sayings and the Epistles in the Bible, are to be studied according to their own literary criticisms. There is no one tool applicable to all the texts of the Bible. So in this sense Narrative Criticism has its limitation.

Critic to Narrative Criticism

Apart from the above difficulty there are serious criticisms raised against Narrative Criticism. It is essential to be aware of them.

i.   Non-historical or a-historical

In Narrative Criticism, narration is claimed "as an event in itself and not the historical occasion in which and to which the text is addressed".[19] In other words, narrative criticism does not care about historicity of the text. But others in Biblical studies hold that the text is also addressed by the historical author to a historical reader. The right perspective will be what Stamps says, "It is one thing to say that narrative criticism cannot be used to extract this historical information; it is another thing to say that such information is unimportant to the interpretation of the text or, more radically, that the text by its very nature as narrative cannot answer such historical questions. Good exegesis cannot ignore historical concerns, even if narrative criticism chooses to".[20] Because one cannot deny the fact that these biblical texts contain history. So Keegan is right when he asks, "Are the Gospels narratives in the same way that novels are narratives?".[21] So what about the history mixed in narration?

ii.   Distorting the Bible

Secondly, some argue against Narrative Criticism saying that in studying the text as literature "we necessarily distort the Bible by speaking of it as literature because it is fundamentally and abidingly a collection of religious documents".[22] Though it is a religious document, the fact is that it contains narration and poetic portions. The right attitude should be that one needs to know narrative criticism even to understand the religious message of the text.

iii. Impossibility of reliability

Some others criticise saying, "what can we really know of the modes of literary communication that were shared by Hebrew storyteller and audience in the early Iron Age?"[23] Alter answers to this critic saying, "despite the historical evolution of literary conventions ... there are also elements of continuity or at least close analogy in the literary modes of disparate ages, and the repertory of narrative devices used by different cultures and eras is hardly infinite".[24]

iv. Incoherencies in the text

One other difficulty with Narrative Criticism is that though it accepts the unity of the text one cannot deny that there is at time 'compositional incoherence'.[25] When there are difficulties in the text that cannot be solved by Narrative Criticism, then one has to have recourse to the composition of the text over the years or centuries.

In *conclusion* we must hold that like any system Narrative Criticism also has its difficulties which are to be solved in individual cases taking recourse to other methods of study. But when one sees the many advantages of Narrative Criticism, one still needs Narrative Criticism to get the full meaning of the text, or the meaning of the author.

Relation with Historical Critical Method

Some may wonder what is the difference between Narrative Criticism and Historical Critical Method to which many of us are introduced and very familiar with? To start with the agreement between Historical Critical Method and Narrative Criticism, we can say, while the former focusses on the *previous history* of the text or formation of the text, the latter concerns the *final stage of the history* of the text i.e., its present form. Studies of Historical Criticism "atomize the story into unrelated literary pieces".[26] This is called by Clines as 'atomism'.[27] The former is diachronic while the latter is synchronic. Another feature of

Historical criticism is geneticism, that is overemphasising the origins and development of the extant Biblical text.

Adele Berlin quotes J. Tigay on how to see the various stages of the text and the place of Narrative Criticism: "For better or worse, however, each writer, compiler, or editor who worked on the epic its forerunners must have had something in mind when he did so. Therefore it seems to me that historical study demands that each version be taken seriously as a piece of literature in its own right and that wherever possible an attempt be made to discern the aims and methods of those who produced it".[28] So ideally it is warranted that the student of an historical text tries to study seriously the text as literature at every stage of its making. But given the reality of complexity of the formation of the text or a book, it is nearly impossible to delineate the texts at every stage and study. So Narrative Criticism takes the final stage of the text seriously and studies it as a literature. This way of doing is more viable and the results are more reliable.

In the Historical Critical Method, "An overemphasis on historical detail cost readers a proper understanding of plot, theme, and character".[29] In other words Historical Criticism "regards the text merely as a 'window' on a world that lies 'behind' the text".[30]

De Boer brings out another difference between Historical Critical Method and Narrative Criticism by the following diagram and by saying, "Historical criticism presupposes real authors and real (first) readers who existed *extrinsic to the text*. Narrative criticism does not; authors and readers exist only *'in the text'*."[31]

Historical criticism

Real Author → Text → Real (first) Reader

Narrative Criticism

Implied Author → Text → Implied Reader

In *conclusion*, the relation between History and literary work in the text can be explained in the words of Paul R. House who summarises the stand point of M. Sternberg, saying, "The Old Testament fuses both what moderns call history and fiction to make ideological points. Historical and literary critics alike must pay attention to the text's historical and artistic components".[32] So both, historical study and artistic study, are important. While Historical Critical Method helps in historical study, Narrative Criticism takes us to the artistic study of the Bible. Therefore the claims of Narrative criticism are very modest. They can be expressed in the words of Kenneth R. R. Gros Louis, "A literary interpretation of the Bible in no way replaces or invalidates other approaches-source analysis, anthropology, sociology, theology, archaeology, comparative religion- nor does it seek to rival in authority the centuries of interpretations in commentaries, or the more recent scholarly contributions of form criticism".[33]

Presuppositions[34]

Narrative Criticism operates on the following assumptions or presuppositions.

a. Universality: As Alter has claimed there is "close analogy" in the literary works of different times.[35] In the words of Tolmie, "Certain characteristics (universals) are found in all narrative texts- from antiquity until modern times".[36] The same is also applicable to Bible as a literary work.

b. Wholeness of the text: The text in the final form is a coherent unity or whole. Narrative Criticism deals with the text as it is.[37] It is taken for granted at least at one stage of its history the text as it stands was taken as unit. It has been also read as a unity down the centuries. So when we do the Narrative Criticism we assume that the final form of the text as we have it today should have been sensible and meaningful for the reader of that time. We want to find out what would have been his/her understanding of the text. So here the text is "an event in itself. The focus is on the experience of the text as a communication event within a specified context".[38] Therefore the text in its final form needs to be examined in its own right. In the words of Paul R. House, "the Bible is a book, and as a book has meaning as a whole that cannot be grasped if an interpreter ignores this point".[39]

c. As corollary to the above presupposition, Narrative criticism does not bother about the *making or history of the text* such as earlier stages of the text; origin and development of the text, namely, the event, oral and written forms, the ideologies that played their role in the making, transmitting, writing and preserving of the event.[40] However, Narrative Criticism does not deny the fact that the text has undergone such a *history/tradition.* Adele Berlin claims, "No literary composition emerges from a vacuum; most borrow something from earlier literature".[41] So at least we grant that it was not a work of single hand. This understanding will come to aid when we come across what Alter calls, "discontinuities, duplications, and contradictions which cannot be so readily accommodated to our own assumptions about literary unity".[42] Only in those instances we may have recourse to Historical Critical Method or Source Criticism.

d. Narrative Criticism *does not venture to reconstruct* the text[43] going back to the period of formation, source, work of the editor etc., for the following two reasons. First, Such a work "can have no easy guarantee of success"[44] because we are separated from the text and its formation nearly by three millennia. There is "enormous distance of intellectual and historical evolution that stands between us and these creations of the early Iron Age".[45] As De Boer puts it, "it is impossible to bring about word-for-word reconstructions of any putative sources and/or prior editions".[46] Second, according to Alter "such insoluble cruxes deriving from the composite nature of the text are a good deal rarer than scholars tend to assume".[47] And the narrative critic should try to explain those cruxes also. To give an example, in the Hagar story the three times repetition of the words, "and the messenger of Yahweh said to her" (vv.9,10, 11) was interpreted by the Historical Critical Method as indication of different sources and the work of an editor of the sources[48] but it can still be interpreted by Narrative Criticism as one unit.[49]

One has to take into account what De Boer says when he quotes de Jonge, "One can never be content with simply describing that history and restrict oneself to the "original" meaning and function of its constituent parts".[50] One has to study the text as a whole because as a whole it 'functioned' at a particular time of history. Those readers "did not take its prehistory into account".[51]

e. The text is interpreted in reference to the implied author and the implied reader as opposed to the real author and the real reader.[52] The text is considered as "a form of communication through which a message is passed from the author to the reader (s)".[53]

f. Affecting lives: Though for many of its readers, Bible is sacred and contains historical narrations, one cannot however deny the fact that these are conveyed in and through one or more literary style. Therefore Bible is also a literary document, though not everything in the Bible is literary in nature, and it has to be studied according to its rules. So Narrative Criticism "assumes conscious artistry in the text". Therefore, as most of the good literary work, and all the more as Scripture, Bible has the creative power of language to affect lives of the individuals and communities.

g. The truth that Narrative Criticism tries to find out is not historical or scientific truth but the truth that the text wants to communicate. So we do not bother, when we read a text, whether it is true in the real world or not. On the contrary, it matters whether it is true "within the fictive world that has been created by the narrative".[54]

This chapter therefore has clarified some of the preliminaries about Narrative Criticism, situating it with other fields of Biblical studies especially Historical Critical Method. Being aware of its limitations and presuppositions, now we pass on to explain some of the basic concepts on which Narrative Criticism operates.

Endnotes

[1] Though the books of Jonas, Esther, Tobit and Judith contain narration, some scholars group it under Midrashic literature which has little of history more of didactic usage.

[2] As quoted by Paul R. House, "The Rise and Current Status of Literary Criticism of the Old Testament" in Paul R. House (ed.,) *Beyond Form Criticism: Essays in Old Testament Literary Criticism*, Winona Lake: Eisenbrauns 1992, 6. Narrative criticism is very much related and close to rhetorical criticism.

[3] Paul R. House, "The Rise and Current Status of Literary Criticism of the Old Testament" in Paul R. House (ed.,), *Beyond Form Criticism: Essays in Old Testament Literary Criticism*, Winona Lake: Eisenbrauns 1992, 6.

[4] D.F. Tolmie, *Narratology and Biblical Narratives. A Practical Guide*, San Francisco: International Scholars Publications, 1999, 1.

[5] D. L. Stamps, "Rhetorical and Narratological Criticism", in Stanly E. Porter (ed.), *Handbook to Exegesis of the New Testament*, Leiden: Brill, 1997, 220.

[6] M.C. de Boer. "Narrative Criticism, Historical Criticism, and the Gospel of John," *JSNT* (1992), 39.

[7] Cf. Kenneth R.R. Gros Louis, "Some Methodological Considerations" in Gross Louis, Kenneth R.R., and Ackermann, James S., (eds.,) *Literary Interpretations of Biblical Narratives* vol. 2 Nashville: Abingdon 1982,17-20.

[8] Cf. Meir Sternberg, *The Poetics of Biblical Narrative: Ideological Literature and the Drama of Reading*, Bloomington: Indiana University Press, 1985, xii.

[9] Robert Alter, *The Art of Biblical Narrative*. New York: Basic Books, 1981, 188.

[10] Shimon Bar-Efrat, *Narrative Art in the Bible*, Dorothea Shefer-Vanson (Trans), Decatur: Almond Press 1989, 9.

[11] Shimon Bar-Efrat, *Narrative Art in the Bible*, Dorothea Shefer-Vanson (Trans), Decatur: Almond Press 1989,10.

[12] Adele Berlin, *Poetics and Interpretation of Biblical Narrative*, Winona Lake, Indiana: Eisenbraus, 1994, 16.

[13] Apart from this there are other tools needed for exegesis such as linguistic knowledge, biblical studies and commentaries.

[14] Robert Alter, *The Art of Biblical Narrative*. New York: Basic Books, 1981, 188.

[15] Paul R. House, "The Rise and Current Status of Literary Criticism of the Old Testament" in Paul R. House (ed.,), *Beyond Form Criticism: Essays in Old Testament Literary Criticism*, Winona Lake: Eisenbrauns 1992, 7.

[16] Paul R. House, "The Rise and Current Status of Literary Criticism of the Old Testament" in Paul R. House (ed.,), *Beyond Form Criticism: Essays in Old Testament Literary Criticism*, Winona Lake: Eisenbrauns 1992, 7.

[17] Robert Alter, *The Art of Biblical Narrative*. New York: Basic Books, 1981, 19.

[18] David M. Gunn, "New Directions in the Study of Biblical Hebrew Narrative" " in Paul R. House (ed.), *Beyond Form Criticism: Essays in Old Testament Literary Criticism*, Winona Lake: Eisenbrauns, 1992, 418.

[19] D. L. Stamps, "Rhetorical and Narratological Criticism", in Stanley E. Porter (ed.), *Handbook to Exegesis of the New Testament*, Leiden: Brill, 1997, 234.

[20] D. L. Stamps, "Rhetorical and Narratological Criticism", in Stanley E. Porter (ed.), *Handbook to Exegesis of the New Testament*, Leiden: Brill, 1997, 235.

[21] Terence J. Keegan, *Interpreting the Bible: A Popular Introduction to Biblical Hermeneutics*, New York: Paulist Press 1985, 106.

[22] R. Alter, "How Convention Helps Us Read: the Case of the Bible's Annunciation Type-Scene" *Prooftexts* 3(1983), 116.

[23] R. Alter, "How Convention Helps Us Read: the Case of the Bible's Annunciation Type-Scene" *Prooftexts* 3(1983), 117.

[24] R. Alter, "How Convention Helps Us Read: the Case of the Bible's Annunciation Type-Scene" *Prooftexts* 3(1983), 117.

[25] Cf. D. L. Stamps, "Rhetorical and Narratological Criticism", in Stanley E. Porter (ed.), *Handbook to Exegesis of the New Testament*, Leiden: Brill, 1997, 236. To name a few, in the background of 1Sam 17:49 and 2 Sam 21:19, who really killed Goliath? Still further, how did really Saul die (cf. 1 Sam 31 and 2 Sam 1)? In the New Testament, which of the four Gospel narrators are reliable? (cf. David M. Gunn, "New Directions in the Study of Biblical Hebrew Narrative" " in Paul R. House (ed.,), *Beyond Form Criticism: Essays in Old Testament Literary Criticism*, Winona Lake: Eisenbrauns 1992, 417). So in the Biblical narration there may be more than one narrator. This gave rise to the Documentary Hypothesis.

[26] D. L. Stamps, "Rhetorical and Narratological Criticism", in Stanley E. Porter (ed.), *Handbook to Exegesis of the New Testament*, Leiden: Brill, 1997, 220-221.

[27] Breaking the text into an excessive number of sources.

[28] As quoted by Adele Berlin, *Poetics and Interpretation of Biblical Narrative*, Winona Lake: Eisenbraus, 1994, 132.

[29] Paul R. House, "The Rise and Current Status of Literary Criticism of the Old Testament" in Paul R. House (ed.,), *Beyond Form Criticism: Essays in Old Testament Literary Criticism*, Winona Lake: Eisenbrauns 1992, 3.

[30] M.C. de Boer. "Narrative Criticism, Historical Criticism, and the Gospel of John," *JSNT* (1992), 42. Regarding the literary criticism of Historical Critical Method, Alter has this to say, "But through the hypothesis of Gattung Gunkel and his followers have sought to determine the so-called life-setting of the various biblical texts, a line of speculation that six

decades of investigation have shown to be highly problematic" (R. Alter, "How Convention Helps Us Read: the Case of the Bible's Annunciation Type-Scene" *Prooftexts* 3(1983), 119.).

[31] M.C. de Boer. "Narrative Criticism, Historical Criticism, and the Gospel of John," *JSNT* (1992), 40. Emphasis added. The terms will be explained in other parts of this book.

[32] Paul R. House, "The Rise and Current Status of Literary Criticism of the Old Testament" in Paul R. House (ed.,), *Beyond Form Criticism: Essays in Old Testament Literary Criticism*, Winona Lake: Eisenbrauns 1992, 17.

[33] Kenneth R.R. Gros Louis, "Some Methodological Considerations" in Kenneth R.R., and Ackermann, James S., (eds.,), *Literary Interpretations of Biblical Narratives*, vol. 2 Gross Louis, Nashville: Abingdon, 1982, 13-14.

[34] Also cf. Kenneth R.R. Gros Louis, "Some Methodological Considerations" in Gross Louis, Kenneth R.R., and Ackermann, James S., (eds.,), *Literary Interpretations of Biblical Narratives*, vol. 2 Nashville: Abingdon 1982, 14-15.

[35] Cf. R. Alter, "How Convention Helps Us Read: the Case of the Bible's Annunciation Type-Scene" *Prooftexts* 3(1983), 117.

[36] D.F. Tolmie, *Narratology and Biblical narratives. A Practical Guide*, San Francisco: International Scholars Publications, 1999,1.

[37] Cf. Meir Sternberg,*The Poetics of Biblical Narrative. Ideological Literature and the Drama of Reading*, Bloomington: Indiana University Press, 1985. p.6-7.

[38] D. L. Stamps, "Rhetorical and Narratological Criticism", in Stanley E. Porter (ed.), *Handbook to Exegesis of the New Testament*, Leiden: Brill, 1997, 229.

[39] Paul R. House, "The Rise and Current Status of Literary Criticism of the Old Testament" in Paul R. House (ed.,), *Beyond Form Criticism: Essays in Old Testament Literary Criticism*, Winona Lake: Eisenbrauns 1992, 17.

[40] Cf. Savina J. Teubal, *Hagar the Egyptian. The Lost Tradition of the Matriarchs*, New York: Harper & Row Publishers, 1990. She however studies Gen 16 from the point of the history and the ideologies that made the text.

[41] Adele Berlin, *Poetics and Interpretation of Biblical Narrative*, Winona Lake: Eisenbraus, 1994, 128.

[42] R. Alter, *The Art of Biblical Narrative*. New York: Basic Books, 1981, 133.

[43] Savina J. Teubal, "Sarah and Hagar: Matriarchs and Visionaries" in Athalya Brenner (ed.) *A Feminist Companion to Genesis,* Sheffield Academic

Press: Sheffield, 1993, 235-250. Idem, *Hagar the Egyptian: The Lost Tradition of the Matriarchs*, New York: Harper & Row Publishers, 1990 and others however have attempted it. According to Teubal for example "only four of the sixteen verses (Gen 16.7-15; 21.14-21) apply to Hagar. The remainder belong to the story of a figure I have identified as the Desert Matriarch."(Savina J. Teubal, "Sarah and Hagar: Matriarchs and Visionaries" in Athalya Brenner (ed.) *A Feminist Companion to Genesis*, Sheffield Academic Press: Sheffield, 1993, 240).

[44] R. Alter, *The Art of Biblical Narrative*. New York: Basic Books, 1981,133.

[45] R. Alter, *The Art of Biblical Narrative*. New York: Basic Books, 1981, 133.

[46] M.C. de Boer. "Narrative Criticism, Historical Criticism, and the Gospel of John," *JSNT*, Vol. 47 (1992), 45.

[47] R. Alter, *The Art of Biblical Narrative*. New York: Basic Books, 1981,133. See there how the author deals the difficulties or internal contradictions in Num 16 and Gen 42.

[48] Cf. Hermann Gunkel, *Genesis*, Göttingen: Vandenhoeck&Ruprecht 1964 in English Biddle, Mark E., *Genesis*, Macon: Mercer University Press, 1997, 183; J. L. Ska, *Abraham Cycle: Synchronic and Diachronic Analysis*, Unpublished class notes, Rome: PIB, 1996, 83.Savina J. Teubal, *Hagar the Egyptian: The Lost Tradition of the Matriarchs*, New York: Harper & Row Publishers, 1990.

[49] Cf. Antony John Baptist, *Together as Sisters: Hagar and Dalit Women*, New Delhi: ISPCK, 2012, 130-131.

[50] M.C. de Boer. "Narrative Criticism, Historical Criticism, and the Gospel of John," *JSNT* Vol. 47 (1992), 36.

[51] M.C. de Boer. "Narrative Criticism, Historical Criticism, and the Gospel of John," *JSNT* Vol. 47 (1992), 37. The terms will be explained latter.

[52] For an explanation of these terms see the next chapter.

[53] D. L. Stamps, "Rhetorical and Narratological Criticism", in Stanley E. Porter (ed.), *Handbook to Exegesis of the New Testament*, Leiden: Brill, 1997, 230.

[54] Kenneth R.R. Gros Louis, "Some Methodological Considerations" in Gross Louis, Kenneth R.R., and Ackermann, James S., (eds.,), *Literary Interpretations of Biblical Narratives*, vol. 2 Nashville: Abingdon 1982, 14.

CHAPTER - 2

Some Basic Concepts

Any text or literary piece of work wants to communicate a message or what I prefer calling ideology, from the sender to the receiver. In this, there is a process of communication. The scholars of Narrative Criticism have broken down that process and refined it into seven elements.[1]

Real author → Implied author → Narrator → Narration → Narratee → Implied reader → Real reader

In addition, Tolmie[2] has elaborated Narration as Characters, Events, Time, Setting, Focalization. Let us try to explain briefly each of the above element.

1. Real Author

Very simply it is "the person(s) who actually wrote the narrative text"[3]. He/she is the real person who wrote the given literary work. In the Biblical narratives it is plurality of persons and in many cases it is unknown.

2. Implied Author

This is "a literary entity that is to be found in the text... authorial person discoverable in the text... distinguishable from the real author."[4] There are two ways of understanding it. Firstly, it can be "the author as implied by the narrative... the idea of the author that is formed in the mind of the reader as s/he reads the narrative text".[5] Ska would define it as, "a projection of the real author into the work".[6] Bar-Efrat explains him/her as "the author who emerges through the story, as opposed to the actual writer".[7] Secondly, it is in terms of the narrative text itself. Tolmie using Chatman defines the implied author as, "the organizing principle in the text, responsible for the total textual arrangement... although the implied author has no direct means of communication (like the narrator), it instructs the reader through the design of the whole text".[8] Stamps quoting Malbon defines the implied author as, "a hypothetical construction based on the requirements of knowledge and belief presupposed in the narrative".[9] The advantage of the idea of the implied author is that "One and the same real author can write a wide variety of different works, each one of which could have a very different implied author".[10] Keegan explains this taking example of Paul and his letters. The implied author of the pastoral letters is indeed very different from the implied author of Romans, but the real author of both is/may be the same.

To arrive at this one needs to study the textual organization of the narrative text, that is, we should study on narrator, narratee, characters, events, time, setting and focalization. After studying all these we will arrive at the overall textual strategy of the implied author. In other words, as a result of our study, we should find out the "specific ideological thrust" or theological thrust of the implied author which s/he wants to impart or to persuade on the implied reader.

3. Narrator

The Narrator is an important element in the narration because the real reader or the implied reader gets the narration from the narrator only. In the words of Tolmie, the voice "within the text is called the narrator... the narrator is a device that is controlled by the implied reader and, that, accordingly, it can be manipulated in various ways by the implied author"[11]. Ska has this to say, "The narrator is always present in the narrative as part of its structure even after the author's death because he is the "voice" that tells the story".[12] For Bar-Efrat, "in narrative the narrator exists alongside the characters".[13] In other words, in any narration, "We do not have direct access to the characters of a narrative, and their speech is even embedded in the narrator's through such phrases as, 'And he said', 'And she answered'. We see and hear only through the narrator's eyes and ears."[14] But we need to distinguish between the feelings of the narrator and the characters. As Bar-Efrat rightly observes, "the biblical narrator tends to imply the feelings of characters through their speech and actions rather than reporting them directly, and that readers have to draw their own conclusions about inner emotions from external behaviour".[15] Fokkelman explains the narrator as "a pose, an attitude... offshoot or a sub-personality of the writer".[16]

In most of the narration the Narrator will not appear directly. There are some indicators of narrator: a. any first-person pronoun that does not designate one of the characters with the narrated world. b. Certain terms such as, "now", "then" "in those days", "there". c. simple phrase like, "he said", d. summeries e. descriptions, f. aetiologies, geographical notes (cf. Gen 16:14), g. sometimes s/he can step out of the story to say something to his audience known as "breaking frame".[17]

That is to say the narrator leaves her/his story for a moment to make a comment about it, as in Gen 16:14.

As regards the presence of the Narrator in Gen 16, we can draw the following conclusions i. In Gen 16:1-6 (act one) we hear the narrator more often than Gen 16:7-14 (act two). ii. In act one, in exposition (v.1) and scene one (vv.2-4) narrator is more constant than in scene two (vv.5-6). iii. In act three we see the narrator often (vv. 15-16).[18] So the narrator is active only at the beginning and at end of the episode and in the main part of the story he/she leaves the narratee to see for himself/herself the development of the story and s/he does not interfere much.

Functions of the Narrator[19]

In any narration the narrator can do any of these three functions.

1. *Directing function*: The Narrator remarks concerning the internal organization of the narrative. This is done by indicating articulations, connections or interrelationships within the narrative text. In Gen 16:1 for example the indication about the barrenness of Sarai, in Gen 16:3 the ten years of sojourn in Canaan can be considered as directing function. The narrator can also "intrude into the story adding comments and explanations" or he can be "silent and self-effacing".[20]

2. *Ideological function*: The narrator may at times explicitly voice out the ideological perspective that s/he wants to communicate to the reader. Some call it 'point of view'. In some cases s/he can be neutral or objective. But in case of the Biblical narrative the former is the case though at times it is not clear. In the words of Fokkelman, "The narrator draws those lines and selects those details, right

down to the smallest, that suit him... He structures time, sketches space, brings characters on and takes them off again, misleads the reader at times, and enforces his point of view through thick and thin".[21] In case of Gen 16 the ideology of the narrator is not explicit in general. But in v.7 where the angel is said to have 'found' Hagar by a spring of water in the wilderness, may indicate the ideological siding of the narrator.[22]

Yet another example can be drawn from Jn 20:30-31 where the narrator makes explicit his/her ideological perspective saying, "Now Jesus did many other signs in the presence of his disciples, which are not written in this book. But these are written so that you may come to believe that Jesus is the Messiah, the Son of God, and that through believing you may have life in his name."(Jn 20:30-31).[23]

3. *Testimonial function:* This is also called function of attestation where the narrator will indicate the sources of his/her information, degree of precision etc. (Cf. 2 Kings 14:18; 15:11; 15:15.).

Kinds of Narrator

The narrator can be an "overt narrator" or a "covert narrator". In other words, s/he can be "dramatized narrator" or "undramatized narrator". The first one is "present as a character or as an explicit, recognizable, 'voice' in the narration."[24] The undramatized narrator is absent. According to Ska, in the Bible the narrator is most of the time invisible, thus undramatized.

Characteristics of the Narrator

In any narration the narrator enjoys some privileges and they are his/her characteristics.[25] The narrator is reliable, omniscient and omnipresent.

Reliable: Though the narrator in other literatures can be reliable or unreliable, in case of Biblical narration it is agreed that the narrator is "straightforwardly reliable".[26] Because the Bible always tells the truth and the narrator who conveys this truth cannot go wrong. Here it does not mean historicity or verifiability of the facts. Rather it means the narrator's views and opinions are accepted without question. This contract between the narrator and the reader is very important in the narrative criticism.

Omniscient: In the words of Bar-Efrat, he/she is "able to see actions undertaken in secret and to hear conversations conducted in seclusion, familiar with the internal workings of the characters and displaying their innermost thoughts to us".[27] Alter explains this in these words, "for the biblical narrator is presumed to know, quite literally, what God knows, as on occasion he may remind us by reposting God's assessments and intentions, or even what He says to Himself".[28] But "...he is highly selective about sharing this omniscience with his readers".[29]

Omnipresent: He is present everywhere. He can report to the reader what has happened in the "cool roof chamber" of Eglon of Moab (cf. Judges 3:20), where there were no one except Ehud and Eglon.

In Gen 16 one could recognize the narrator in v.1 where he begins the narration with the word "now", and in v.7 where the angel of the Lord 'found' Hagar (ideological function) and the whole v.14 in the aetiology of Beer-lahai-roi. The omniscience of the narrator is clear in reporting the dialogue between Sarai and Abram (cf. v.2 and v.6) and the conversation between the angel of the Lord and Hagar in the wilderness (cf. v. 8-12) and Hagar giving name to God (cf. v.13).

Level and Relation between Narrator and the Narration[30]

Firstly, in the case of level of narration, the narrator can be outside or inside the story. Secondly, in the case of relationship, the narrator can tell his/her own story or the story of somebody else. Thus there are four possibilities.

1. An external narrator telling the story of somebody else (eg. from Gen to 2 Kings, Gen 16; the Gospels).

2. An external narrator tells his own story in the first person (Nehemiah; Ecclesiastes; Ezra 7:27-9:15; Tob 1:3-3:6; Isa 6; Jer 1; Ez 1-3).

3. A narrator within the story telling a story or stories from which s/he is absent (eg. the parables; Judg 9:7-15; 2Sam 12:1-4).

4. A narrator within the story telling his own story (Acts 22:1-21; 26:1-23).

4. Narration

This can be also said to be the text. In the narration the authoritative knowledge of the narrator extends from the beginning. He narrates the story. Therefore as said earlier, "He (narrator) is all-knowing and also perfectly reliable: at times he may choose to make us wonder but he never misleads us"[31]. As the reader reads the story s/he has to ask some questions such as, why is a motive or feeling attributed to one character and not to another? Why is one character's attitude toward another stated flatly in one instance, both stated and explained in a second instance, and entirely withheld from us in a third? Why at a particular juncture does the narrator break the time-frame of his story to insert a piece of expository information in the pluperfect tense, or to jump forward to the time of his contemporary audience and explain that in those days it was the custom in Israel to perform such and such a practice? (Cf. Gen 16: 14). David Gunn and D.N. Fewell think, "The power of narrative lies in its ability to imitate life, to evoke a world that is like ours, to reproduce like-like events and situations, to recreate people that we understand and to whom relate. And we become acquainted with these people in much the same way we get to know people in real life".[32]

Modes of Narration

There are two modes of narration. The first one is to tell the reader what happened or *telling* the implied/real reader what to think of the character. Here the reliable narrator directly speaks to the reader. The second one is *showing* them the scene and letting the reader judge for him/herself.[33] In case of Gen 16 it is more of showing and little of telling. So the reader has to be attentive and alert to see what the implied author is showing. Especially the implied author could not tell many things about Hagar because of the cultural context of existence of Slavery of his/her time but s/he beautifully shows the character of Hagar using various devices. So we need to find out the voice of the narrator and his/her strategy and ideology in the narration. This is the whole goal of our exegesis.

The narration contains other elements such as Characters, Events, Time, Setting and Focalization. These will be dealt in detail in the next chapter.[34] For the time being a list of *various narrative techniques* can be listed from Alter which run as follows: "the deployment of thematic key-words; the reiteration of motifs; the subtle definition of character, relations, and motives mainly through dialogue; the exploitation, especially in dialogue, of verbatim repetition with minute but significant changes introduced; the narrator's discriminating shifts from strategic and suggestive withholding of comment to the occasional flaunting of an omniscient overview; the use at points of a montage of sources to catch the multifaceted nature of the fictional subject".[35]

5. Narratee

Narratee is "one or more persons within the text to whom the narrator tells his/her story. This intra textual listener(s) is (are) called the narratee"[36]. In simple terms the narrator is telling the story to the narratee. As Keegan says "in most of the cases the narratee is unnamed and does not appear anywhere in the story".[37] But there are some indicators thorough which the narratee can be recognized. They are a. a second person pronoun that does not refer to a character (s) within the narrated world. b. sometimes a first person plural may refer both narrator and the narratee, c. reference to the knowledge or attitude. We can see the narratee in v.7 in the information about the place -the spring on the way to Shur. It refers to the knowledge of the reader about this place. For the same reason v.14 (Beer-lahai-roi which lies between Kadesh and Bered.) can also be seen as presence of the narratee.

6. Implied Reader

There are again two opinions about the implied reader. The first one, s/he is "the reader that the real author had in mind when s/he wrote the text or the kind of real reader presupposed by the text".[38] Secondly, "it can be depersonified and instead be linked closely to the text itself."[39] It is "an intratextual literary construct, functioning as a counterpart of the implied author".[40] He/she is reader implied by the text. What Ska says of implied reader seems to be simple and clear. The implied reader is no one other than "the real reader, who accepts the contract proposed by the implied author, 'becomes' the implied reader…is less a person than a role that every concrete reader is invited to perform in the act of reading".[41] That is, "there are certain presuppositions made by the text concerning the reader. There are certain directives given to the reader, certain expectations made of the reader".[42] Therefore the text calls for certain commitments and values on the part of the reader. Once s/he accepts that s/he becomes the 'implied reader'. S/he has to fulfil the role presupposed by the text. To the extent he/she does it to that extent "people make a strong commitment of their very persons to the act of reading and come to know themselves more deeply".[43] Thus the text, especially the Scriptures, has an effect on the reader.

So by now it would have been clear that there are two worlds in the reading process, real world of the events narrated and narrative world.[44] As Keegan explains, "The narrative world is not the real world. The real world in which real people live and move and have their being is unbounded in space and time".[45] The narrative world though look like the real world it is limited by the narrator.

Three reading positions

In the process of reading a text there are three reading positions possible depending upon "levels of knowledge possessed by the characters and the reader."[46] They are 1. reader elevating, that means, the reader knows more than the character(s), (most of the theophanies fall in this group: cf. Gen 18:1-15 – the reader knows that the Lord appears to Abraham; Gen 22:1-19 the reader knows that God tests Abraham; Ex 3:1-6 the reader knows that the angel of the Lord appears to Moses; also cf.

Judg 6:11-24; 13:2-25; Gen 4:9; Gen 19:30-38; Gen 18:12; Gen 27; Gen 31:31-32; Gen 38; Gen 43-45; Ex 5:2; Num 22:22-31; Josh 9; Judg 11:34-35), 2. character elevating - the character(s) know(s) more than reader (Gen 29:15-19 – the plan of Laban; Judg 3:12-30 – the intention of Ehud; 2 Sam 14:1-24 – the plan of Joab; Jon 1:3 - Jonah's flight), and 3. even handed - both reader and character(s) have the same level of knowledge (cf. Gen 22 – Abraham's attempt to sacrifice Isaac; Gen 38 – Judah and Tamar).

As in most of the theophanies in case of the Hagar episode also we have reader-elevating position. Because the reader is informed already in v.7 that the messenger of Yahweh is speaking to Hagar and in v.10 it is Yahweh who is speaking ("Indeed I will cause to multiply your offspring") but Hagar realises it only in v.13. But for this one element the rest of the story is in even handed position where both the reader and the character(s) discover the unfolding of the events and the plot keeps the narrative tension up all through the narrative.

Three reader's interests

A good story arouses interests in the implied reader. They are of three kinds:

1. Intellectual or cognitive: This means intellectual curiosity; interest for truth.

2. Qualitative: desire to see any pattern or form completed; interest for beauty.

3. Practical: " a strong desire for the success or failure of those we love or hate, admire or detest, or we can be made to hope for or fear a change in the quality of a character".[47] This can also be called 'human interest'. It is interest for goodness.

I think that the Hagar episode will very well fall in the third group. Though the reader is neutral at the beginning of the episode, he/she is confused whether to support or oppose the reaction of Hagar after her pregnancy. S/he takes side with Hagar when s/he knows that Abram, her husband, had given her to the hand of Sarai and that Sarai afflicted her. This stance of the reader is confirmed when the messenger of Yahweh appears to her and speaks to her the message of hope. So the interest of reader in the Hagar episode is 'human interest' or 'interest for goodness'. Ska explicitly refers to this episode and says, "Hagar is a figure who deserves much sympathy. Even the angel of God tries to restore justice on her behalf (Gen 16, 9-12; 21, 17-20) (practical interest)"[48]. However seen from the main plot line in Genesis she has only a secondary role (cognitive interest).

7. Real reader

The Real reader is "the actual person who is reading the narrative text."[49] The Real author and the real reader exist "in the world outside of and independent of the text".[50]

Diagram of Keegan[51] correctly locates the seven elements in the real world and narrative world (the text). So I reproduce the diagram here. What he calls as Narrative Expression we call as Narration.[52]

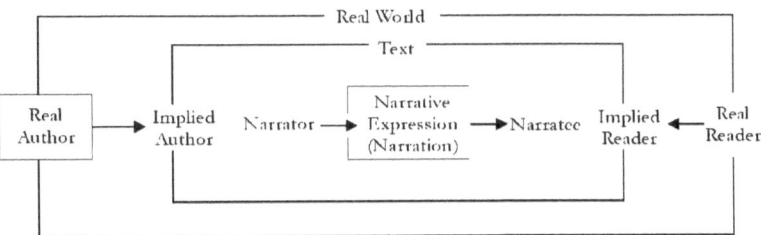

Conclusion

This chapter tried to clarify some of the basic concepts involved in the reading process, such as Real author, Implied author, Narrator, Narratee, Implied reader, Real reader. Now remains the Narration in which we find elements such as Characters, Events, Time, Setting and Focalization.[53] These will be studied in the following chapters.[54]

Endnotes

[1] Cf. J. L. Ska, *"Our Fathers Have Told Us" Introduction to the Analysis of Hebrew Narratives.* (SubBib 13) Rome: PIB Press, 1990, 40. There is also a diagram available in Terence J.Keegan, *Interpreting the Bible: A Popular Introduction to Biblical Hermeneutics*, New York: Paulist Press 1985, 94. He replaces Narration with Narrative Expression.

[2] Cf. D.F. Tolmie, *Narratology and Biblical narratives. A Practical Guide*, San Francisco: International Scholars Publications, 1999, 6.

[3] D.F. Tolmie, *Narratology and Biblical narratives. A Practical Guide*, San Francisco: International Scholars Publications, 1999, 6.

[4] Terence J. Keegan, *Interpreting the Bible: A Popular Introduction to Biblical Hermeneutics*, New York: Paulist Press 1985, 95.

[5] D.F. Tolmie, *Narratology and Biblical narratives. A Practical Guide*, San Francisco: International Scholars Publications, 1999, 6.

[6] J. L. Ska, *"Our Fathers Have Told Us" Introduction to the Analysis of Hebrew Narratives.* (SubBib 13) Rome: PIB Press, 1990, 41.

[7] Shimon Bar-Efrat, *Narrative Art in the Bible*, Dorothea Shefer-Vanson (Trans), Decatur: Almond Press 1989, 14.

[8] D.F. Tolmie, *Narratology and Biblical narratives. A Practical Guide*, San Francisco: International Scholars Publications, 1999, 7.

[9] As quoted by D. L. Stamps, "Rhetorical and Narratological Criticism", in Stanley E. Porter (ed.), *Handbook to Exegesis of the New Testament*, Leiden: Brill, 1997, 229.

[10] Terence J. Keegan, *Interpreting the Bible: A Popular Introduction to Biblical Hermeneutics*, New York: Paulist Press 1985, 95.

[11] D.F. Tolmie, *Narratology and Biblical narratives. A Practical Guide*, San Francisco: International Scholars Publications, 1999, 13. Narrator is only a functional construct.

[12] J. L. Ska, *"Our Fathers Have Told Us" Introduction to the Analysis of Hebrew Narratives*, (SubBib 13) Rome: PIB Press, 1990, 44.

[13] Shimon Bar-Efrat, *Narrative Art in the Bible*, Dorothea Shefer-Vanson (Trans), Decatur: Almond Press, 1989, 13.

[14] Shimon Bar-Efrat, *Narrative Art in the Bible*, Dorothea Shefer-Vanson (Trans), Decatur: Almond Press 1989, 13.

[15] Shimon Bar-Efrat, *Narrative Art in the Bible*, Dorothea Shefer-Vanson (Trans), Decatur: Almond Press 1989, 18. That is why the difference between the narrator text and character text is important (cf. chapter four on Textual Strategy). However the same author also shows how the narrator can penetrate into the minds of the character.

[16] J.P. Fokkelman, *Reading Biblical Narrative: An Introductory Guide*, Louisville: Westminster John Knox Press 1999, 55.

[17] Cf. Adele Berlin, *Poetics and Interpretation of Biblical Narrative*, Winona Lake: Eisenbraus, 1994, 57.

[18] The ideas can be presented in the form of diagram as follows

Act one

Exposition (v.1)	narrator's presence is more
Scene one (vv.2-4)	narrator's presence is more
Scene two (vv.5-6)	narrator's presence is less

Act two

Scene one (vv. 7-14)	narrator's presence is less
Scene two (v. 15)	narrator's presence is more
Conclusion (v.16)	narrator's presence is more

[19] Fokkelman lists some of the basic communications that the narrator uses or complies with as 1. remain attractive, 2. easy to follow (followability), 3.diversity of data (people, acts, words, motives, points of view, intentions, Cf. J.P. Fokkelman, *Reading Biblical Narrative: An Introductory Guide* Louisville: Westminster John Knox Press, 1999, 55-56.).

[20] Shimon Bar-Efrat, *Narrative Art in the Bible*, Dorothea Shefer-Vanson (Trans), Decatur: Almond Press, 1989, 14.

[21] J.P. Fokkelman, *Reading Biblical Narrative: An Introductory Guide* Louisville: Westminster John Knox Press 1999, 55. He even says "a sound narratology is largely a form of rhetorical analysis" (Ibid., 56).

[22] In situations like this, the usual expressions are "called to him from heaven" (Gen 22:11; 22:15), 'appeared' (Ex 3:2), or 'took his stand' (Num

22:22). The use of 'found' instead would mean that God was searching for her. The scholars are however divided on interpreting this searching and finding. For discussion on this ref. my book, *Together as Sisters*, New Delhi: ISPCK, 2012, 128-129. I have interpreted it as positive, as God having special concern for Hagar, searching 'with compassion and anxiety, in the moment of her personal suffering.'

[23] Unless stated otherwise the quotes from the Bible are from NRSV of Bible works version 7.

[24] J. L. Ska, *"Our Fathers Have Told Us" Introduction to the Analysis of Hebrew Narratives*, (SubBib 13) Rome: PIB Press, 1990, 45.

[25] Cf. Gunn, D.M and Fewell, D.N., *Narrative in the Hebrew Bible*, Oxford: Oxford University Press. 1993, 53. As the author of literary work he also has *poetic license*. So much so Fokkelman even says "in narrative texts God is a character, i.e. a creation of the narrator and writer... The narrator decides whether God is allowed to say anything in the story and if so, how often and how much" (cf. J.P. Fokkelman, *Reading Biblical Narrative: An Introductory Guide* Louisville: Westminster John Knox Press 1999, 58).

[26] Meir Sternberg, *The Poetics of Biblical Narrative: Ideological Literature and the Drama of Reading*, Bloomington: Indiana University Press, 1985, 51. Also cf. D.F. Tolmie, *Narratology and Biblical narratives. A Practical Guide*, San Francisco: International Scholars Publications, 1999, 21.

[27] Shimon Bar-Efrat, *Narrative Art in the Bible*, Dorothea Shefer-Vanson (Trans), Decatur: Almond Press 1989, 17. Also cf. J.P. Fokkelman, *Reading Biblical Narrative: An Introductory Guide* Louisville: Westminster John Knox Press 1999, 56.

[28] R. Alter, *The Art of Biblical Narrative*, New York: Basic Books, 1981,157. Also cf. J. L. Ska, *"Our Fathers Have Told Us" Introduction to the Analysis of Hebrew Narratives,* (SubBib 13) Rome: PIB Press, 1990, 44; Terence J. Keegan, *Interpreting the Bible: A Popular Introduction to Biblical Hermeneutics*, New York: Paulist Press 1985, 100; 2Sam 12:1; Gen 6:6.

[29] R. Alter, *The Art of Biblical Narrative*. New York: Basic Books, 1981, 158.

[30] Cf. J. L. Ska, *"Our Fathers Have Told Us" Introduction to the Analysis of Hebrew Narratives*, (SubBib 13) Rome: PIB Press, 1990, 46-47.

[31] R. Alter, *The Art of Biblical Narrative*. New York: Basic Books, 1981, 184.

[32] D.M. Gunn, and, D.N. Fewell, *Narrative in the Hebrew Bible*Oxford: OxfordUniversity Press. 1993, 47.

[33] Cf. J. L. Ska, *"Our Fathers Have Told Us" Introduction to the Analysis of Hebrew Narratives.* (SubBib 13) Rome: PIB Press, 1990, 53; M. A. Powell, *What is Narrative Criticism?* London: SPCK, 1993, 52.

[34] Added to that, we will also discuss about the words and dialogue.

[35] R. Alter, *The Art of Biblical Narrative.* New York: Basic Books, 1981, 176.

[36] D.F. Tolmie, *Narratology and Biblical narratives. A Practical Guide*, San Francisco: International Scholars Publications, 1999, 13.

[37] Terence J. Keegan, *Interpreting the Bible: A Popular Introduction to Biblical Hermeneutics*, New York: Paulist Press 1985, 101.

[38] D.F. Tolmie, *Narratology and Biblical narratives. A Practical Guide*, San Francisco: International Scholars Publications, 1999, 8.

[39] D.F. Tolmie, *Narratology and Biblical narratives. A Practical Guide*, San Francisco: International Scholars Publications, 1999, 8.

[40] D.F. Tolmie, *Narratology and Biblical narratives. A Practical Guide*, San Francisco: International Scholars Publications, 1999, 8.

[41] J. L. Ska, *"Our Fathers Have Told Us" Introduction to the Analysis of Hebrew Narratives,* (SubBib 13) Rome: PIB Press, 1990, 42-43.

[42] Terence J. Keegan, *Interpreting the Bible: A Popular Introduction to Biblical Hermeneutics,* New York: Paulist Press 1985, 96.

[43] Terence J. Keegan, *Interpreting the Bible: A Popular Introduction to Biblical Hermeneutics,* New York: Paulist Press 1985, 97. He even goes to the level of saying that becoming an implied reader involves "becoming a slave of the text, becoming slave of the ideology involved in the text" (p.97). Applying this to Biblical texts he says, "only a believer can assume the role of the implied reader of a biblical text" (Terence J. Keegan, *Interpreting the Bible: A Popular Introduction to Biblical Hermeneutics,* New York: Paulist Press 1985, 98).

[44] Cf. Terence J. Keegan, *Interpreting the Bible: A Popular Introduction to Biblical Hermeneutics,* New York: Paulist Press 1985, 94 (diagram) and 102 - 104.

[45] Terence J. Keegan, *Interpreting the Bible: A Popular Introduction to Biblical Hermeneutics,* New York: Paulist Press 1985, 102.

[46] J. L. Ska, *"Our Fathers Have Told Us" Introduction to the Analysis of Hebrew Narratives,* (SubBib 13) Rome: PIB Press, 1990, 54.

[47] J. L. Ska, *"Our Fathers Have Told Us" Introduction to the Analysis of Hebrew Narratives,* (SubBib 13) Rome: PIB Press, 1990, 62.

[48] J. L. Ska, *"Our Fathers Have Told Us" Introduction to the Analysis of Hebrew Narratives*, (SubBib 13) Rome: PIB Press, 1990, 62.

[49] D.F. Tolmie, *Narratology and Biblical narratives. A Practical Guide*, San Francisco: International Scholars Publications, 1999, 6.

[50] Terence J. Keegan, *Interpreting the Bible: A Popular Introduction to Biblical Hermeneutics*, New York: Paulist Press 1985, 93.

[51] Cf. Terence J. Keegan, *Interpreting the Bible: A Popular Introduction to Biblical Hermeneutics*, New York: Paulist Press 1985, 94.

[52] Tolmie also give a diagram (Cf. D.F. Tolmie, *Narratology and Biblical narratives. A Practical Guide*, San Francisco: International Scholars Publications, 1999, 6.). There he elaborates the Narrative Expression (Narration) further as Characters, Events, Time, Setting and Focalization.

[53] I also include words and dialogue in this list.

[54] Focalization will be discussed in chapter four: The implied author's textual strategy.

CHAPTER - 3

The Narration of the Text

The above chapters prepared us the way to read the text, explaining some concepts. But the real and important thing is to read the text. So this chapter deals about the elements that are found in the text and how to approach them to understand the message the implied author wants to communicate through the text.

In any narrative, Bar-Efrat finds three strata "1. the stratum of language – the words and sentences of which the narrative is composed; 2. the stratum of what is represented by those words, namely the 'world' described in the narrative: the characters, events and settings; Powell explains these three as, "Somebody does something to someone, somewhere, at sometime. The 'something' that is done is an event, the 'somebody' and 'someone' are characters, and the 'somewhere' and 'sometime' are settings.[1] 3. the stratum of meanings, that is the concepts, views and values embodied in the narrative, which are expressed principally through the speech and actions of the characters, their fate and the general course of events".[2] So the elements involved in the text are *Characters, Events/*

actions, Time, Setting, words, dialogue, and narration. Let us try to understand some basic ideas about each of them.

1. CHARACTERS

In reading the narration in the text, sometimes "the characters are quite capable of lying and deceit". So we should not believe what the character says. How to find it out whether a particular character is deceiving or not? 1. In the narration the narrator shares with the reader his omniscience or prior knowledge. Basing on that we can decide on the truthfulness of the character. 2. By comparing the words of the character with his/her actions we can find it out. If they speak well but do atrocities we give in to the actions and not to the words. This is seen in the character of Sarai. What she speaks in v.2 is honey but what she does in v.6 is wicked. 3. Sometimes the narrator through interventions directly tells the reader that the character is deceiving or lying. We should be very careful in judging the characters. As mentioned earlier, the narrator is not so. The narrator in the narration has to be believed and accepted.

2. EVENTS/ACTIONS

Events "are the incidents or happenings that occur within a story".[3] They consist of speech, thoughts, feelings and perceptions. Actions, according to Fokkelman, helps for the grasping of the story and to make a summary.[4] He also presents the various elements of actions: 1. Deeds the characters perform. They are in active forms and the characters are responsible for them.[5] 2. There is an enduring aspect that is in passive form.[6] 3. Descriptive and explanatory sentences, through which, "the narrator offers some background, sketches a situation, or reveals motives or purposes"[7] 4. Processes which include coordination of time and space.

Kinds of Actions

There are two types of actions according to their importance.

1. Kernels: These are actions that are "so essential that they could not possibly be removed without destroying the logic of the narrative".[8] Here choices are made and these determine the subsequent development. 2. Satellites: These actions "could conceivably be deleted without disturbing the basic plot".[9] These do not involve choices but simply describe.

In judging and understanding the events or actions narrated in the text, we need to keep in mind the following:

i. Recurrence

By this we mean those themes that occur again and again in the narrative. For example, the deflection of primogeniture is spoken of many times in Genesis (cf. Gen 10:15; 19:31, 33, 34, 37; 22:21; 25:13; 27:19, 32; 29:36; 35:23; 36:15; 38:6, 7; 41:51; 43:33; 46:8; 48:14, 18; 49:3). These can be considered also as a *Leitwort* or Motif.

ii. Parallels/ repeated actions

This means two versions of the same event. Sometimes in the Biblical Narration the same event, with minor variations, occurs at different junctures of the narrative, usually involving different characters or sets of characters. In this case we should ask "why he (writer) should have done this, in what ways do the two narrative perspectives complement or complicate each other."[10] The two Hagar episodes in Gen 16:1-16 and Gen 21:9-21 can be one example of parallels and repeated actions. First time when Hagar was pregnant and other time when Ishmael and Isaac were born. The multiplication of bread by Jesus in the Gospels (cf. feeding of the five thousand Mt 14:13-21; Mk 6:32-44; Lk 9:10-17; Jn 6:1-15; feeding of the four thousand Mt 15:32-39; Mk 8:1-10) can be another example. In such cases we have to watch for the minute and often revelatory changes that a given scene undergoes as it passes from one place to another.[11]

iii. Concatenation (series of interconnections)

There is, among the Biblical narrations, "a causal chain that firmly connects one event to the next, link by link."[12] For example there is a link between Gen 21 and Gen 22, where the son of Abram, Isaac, is in danger.

3. TIME

We need to distinguish basically between objective time and narrated time. "Objective time is continuous and flows evenly without interruptions, delays or accelerations (provided the speed of the measuring mechanism remains constant), advancing in a straight line and an orderly fashion from the past via the present to the future. It is also irreversible".[13] Narrative time "is subjective and expands or contracts according to the circumstances; it is never continuous, being subject to gaps, delays and jump, nor does it display the meticulous division into past, present and future... Narrated time is not uniform or regular and its directions and speed often change."[14] The narrator can exploit this time according to his intention and purpose to the story/episode.

In discussing on time we should also speak of i. Order, ii. Duration, iii. Frequency[15] iv. Temporal expressions, v. Time Stop and vi. Psychological Time.

i. Order of Time

Here the question is "are events in a narrative always presented in which they occur?"[16] In the biblical narrative generally there is agreement between the order of narrated time (the order in which events happened) and that of narration time (the order in which they are narrated). One technique used for this is *waw*, translated as, 'and'. In Gen 16 for example all the verses (except v.14) begin with the *waw*, so that the episode flows in one direction. There are however instances (also in biblical narrative) where time is reversed for some reason. They can be of two ways[17] 1. Flashback (*analepsis*): Bar- Efrat explains it saying, "the function of flashback is to recount what has happened meanwhile somewhere else or to someone other than the characters with which the narrative has been dealing".[18] For example Judg 11:1-3 is a flashback where the birth and the growth of Jephthah are narrated. Then Judg 11:4 recounts the story and connects to the last verse of Judg 10 where Ammonites were ready for war (also cf. 1 Kings 1:6; 11: 14-22, 23-25). 2. anticipation (*prolepsis*): This on the other hand, "when the narrator wishes to hint at what is to come this is done as an organic part of the action. One of the participants in the plot who has the capacity to see into the future – whether a prophet, an angel of the Lord or even God himself (either directly by means of a dream) – informs one of the other participants of events which are about to occur... It sheds light on the deeper meaning of what is happening, enabling us concurrently with reading about the events, to transcend them, grasp the causal connections between them and perceive the hidden forces behind them".[19] The message of the messenger in Gen 16: 11-12 (namely the birth of Ishmael and his character) can be said as anticipation.[20]

As regards the relationship between the process of narration and the story that happened, there are four types possible i. Ulterior (narrated after the event, Gen 16 falls in this group), ii. anterior (narrated before the event), iii. Simultaneous iv. Intercalated (narrated alternately).[21]

ii. Duration[22]

This means assessing the 'speed' of the narrative, by comparing Narrative time and narration time. Tolmie calls them 'story time' and 'text time'.

a. Narrative time or story time or Erzähltezeit

This "is the duration of the actions and events in the story".[23] It is measured in units of "real" time (seconds, minutes, hours, days, months, years, centuries, millenaries).[24]

b. Narration time or text time or Erzählzeit

This "is material time necessary to tell (or peruse) the "discourse" (concrete narrative). Here the "duration" is the length of the narrative and it is measured in words, sentences, lines, verses, paragraphs, pages, chapters".[25]

When these two times are established then we need to compare them to fix the "slowdowns or accelerations in the narrative text"[26]. According to Tolmie five types of relationships are possible between story-time (ST) and text time (TT).[27]

i. Narrative Pause: Narration of something without a corresponding segment in the story; $TT=n$, $ST=0$; TT infinitely $>ST$. "The narrator takes "time out" to describe or explains something to the reader and then picks up the story again where he or she left off".[28] Gen 16:14 can be considered as narrator's "time out".

ii. Slowdown/ Stretch (according to Powell[29]): Here the text time devoted to the narration of the event seems to be longer than the length of time that the event took to occur. This can be represented as TT>ST.

iii. Scenic representation: The duration of events in the narrative text and the duration of events in the story seem to be more or less identical which is like this: TT=ST. Dialogues are "purest form of scenic representation"[30]. The ratio here is approximately 1:1 (cf. Gen 16:7-13 - dialogue between Hagar and the messenger of God).

iv. Summary: This means that the narrative text is condensed and fill a shorter space in the text than would have been the case if it had been presented by means of scenic representation. This means TT<ST. According to Bar-Efrat "When action is included in a scene its duration is longer than narration time"[31] (cf. Gen 22:9; Gen 16:3-4, 7, 15).

v. Ellipsis: The event is not narrated in the narrative text although it is clear that it must have occurred at the story level. TT=0, ST=n. Here "the reader assumes that several hours have passed in the world of the story, even though the discourse of the narrative does not report this".[32] In this sense Gen 16:4 (Sarai becoming little in the sight of Hagar) and Gen 16:6 (affliction of Hagar by Sarai) can be seen as Ellipsis.

Now the question is how to find out the emphasis of the author. Where does s/he want to focus our attention in the vast area of narration? As a general rule, the scenic representation is the place where the emphasis of the author lies. According to Bar-Efrat "If we note the variations in narrated time in relation to narration time ranging from scenic representation to summary account, we will discover the narrative's focal points and the relative importance of its various subjects."[33] So in Gen 16 we can say the focal point is in vv.7-12 where we have a scenic representation. But the time passes rapidly in the account of Act one (Gen 16:1-6). Bar-Efrat gives a general tendency in biblical narrative, "the preparations preceding events and the reactions following them as being more important than the events themselves, denoting a special interest in matters pertaining to the human mind, its motives, decisions and attitudes. In other words, the human aspects, whether psychological, spiritual or moral, are granted greater emphasis than factual components".[34] In Gen 16:1-6 we can see v.4 (the reaction of Hagar after becoming pregnant) as the main action and the previous and latter events as preparation and effect respectively. So it would demand that we study the psychological, spiritual or moral aspect of the reaction of Hagar rather than anything else.[35]

As an exercise, let us try to apply the duration of time to Gen 16 and find out the narrative time and narration time. This will help us to find out or locate the choice or emphasis of the narrator. For measuring the narration time we use BibliaHebraicaStuttgartensia, Stuttgart: Deutsche Bibelgesellschaft, 4th edition, 1990 as basic text. For narrative time in the following analysis it is only approximate and it can be disputed.

	Story time	Text time
Act one		
Exposition (v.1)	————	one line
Scene one (v.2-4)		
Sarai's proposal (v.2a)	few days[36]	one and half lines

Abram's response (v.2b)	few minutes/ one day	four words
Sarai's action (v.3)	one day	two lines
Hagar's reaction (v.4)	few months[37]	one line[38]
Scene two (vv. 5-6)		
Sarai's complaint (v.5)	few minutes	two lines
Abram's response (v.6a)	few minutes	one line
Sarai's action (v.6b)	few days/months	two words
Hagar's reaction (v.6c)	one day[39]	two words

Act two (vv.7-14)

Messenger finding Hagar at the well (v.7)	few minutes/hours	one line
Hagar's reply to the messenger (v.8)	"	one and a half line
Words of messenger - Return (v.9)	"	one line
Words of messenger- Multitude of descendants (v.10)	"	one line
Words of messenger – birth and future of Ishmael (vv. 11-12)	"	five lines
Hagar's exclamation (v.13)	"	one and half line
Well is named (v.14)	——————	one line

Act three (v.15-16)

Hagar comes to give birth (v.15a)	few months[40]	three words
Abram gives name (v.15b)	few minutes	six words
Age of Abram (v.16)	—————[41]	one line

Basing on the above table, the possible relation between story time and text time can be formulated as follows.

- In case of the exposition (v.1) there is narration time but there is no corresponding action in the story time. TT infinitely $> ST$[42]

- In scene one there are two things involved.

i. In v.2 there is scenic representation where TT and ST are more or less identical: $TT=ST$[43]

ii. In vv. 3-4 there is a summary where "the narrative text are condensed and fill a shorter space in the text than would have been the case if they had been presented by means of scenic representation":[44] $TT<ST$.

- The same thing can be said of scene two. That is to say vv. 5-6a is scenic representation: $TT=ST$ and v. 6b-6c is summary: $TT<ST$

- In *Act two, scene one*, in comparison to other scenes, the action is slowed down. That is to say, "the length of text-time devoted to the narration of the event seems to be longer than the length of time that the event took to occur"[45]. So $TT>ST$. While in the previous and in the following scenes the events that last for days and months are summarized or narrated in few words or lines, in this *scene one*, a scene that would have lasted for few minutes or an hour is narrated in 12 lines. In other words the textual time of this scene one is equal to the textual time of all other scenes, exposition and conclusion. Therefore this scene can be regarded as very important by the implied author.[46] So this scene has to be studied carefully to understand the ideological or theological content or argument of the narrator (or implied author). It is here the narrator (implied author) will come out with his/her own ideology.

- Scene two of act two also can be viewed as summary where textual time is less than story time.

- The conclusion of the episode like the exposition is narrative pause where there is textual time without any story time. That is to say TT infinitely >ST.

iii. Frequency

This means "the number of times an event occurs in the "story level" and the number of times it is narrated in the narrative text".[47] There are three kinds of frequency possible.

A. singular frequency: It is a one-to-one relationship i.e., "an event that happened once is narrated once; or the same kind of event that happened more than once is narrated a corresponding number of times"[48]. Powell would call the second one as Multiple-singular narration.[49] The Hagar story as narrated in Gen 16 should have happened only once and it is narrated only once.

B. Repetitive frequency: What happened once is narrated more than once in the narrative text.[50]

C. Iterative frequency: What happened more than once is narrated once in the narrative text.

iv. Temporal Expressions

There are two kinds of temporal expressions possible.

1. Expressions denoting duration: For example "The rain fell on the earth forty days and forty nights." (Gen 7:12); "So Jacob served seven years for Rachel, and they seemed to him but a few days because of the love he had for her." (Gen 29:20); "The time that the Israelites had lived in Egypt was four hundred thirty years. " (Ex 12:40); "So, after Abram had lived ten years in the land of Canaan..." (Gen 16:3).

2. Expressions denoting points of time: The following can be stated as examples: "He made the camels kneel down outside the city by the well of water; it was toward evening, the time when women go out to draw water." (Gen 24:11); "So Gideon and the hundred who were with him came to the outskirts of the camp at the beginning of the middle watch, when they had just set the watch; and they blew the trumpets and smashed the jars that were in their hands." (Judg 7:19); "Then at the break of dawn Samuel called to Saul upon the roof" (1 Sam 9:26). In Gen 16 the mention of age of Abram in v. 16 can also be grouped here.

v. Time Stop

Time stops in two situations: 1. when interpretations, explanations, conclusions or evaluations are given. For example "Therefore the well was called Beer-lahai-roi; it lies between Kadesh and Bered. ... Abram was eighty-six years old when Hagar bore him Ishmael."(Genesis 16:14,16) 2. When depictions are given within the narrative (cf. Gen 16:1).

vi. Psychological Time

By this "what is meant is the pace of time, the rate at which it proceeds with regard to the reader's subjective feeling… Monotony slows it down while interest and suspense speed it up".[51] Bar-Efrat has this to say about biblical narratives, "Most biblical narratives are full of tension, containing numerous unusual events, dramatic incidents, sharp contrasts and fierce clashes. One crisis follows another, the characters become involved in complex situations and the reader eagerly awaits the disentangling of the threads. Everything is extremely dynamic, purposeful and condensed, and the reader's attention is always focused on what is to follow … All these elements operate to create a rapid psychological pace".[52] Most of these can be very well applied to Gen 16:1-6. The psychological time in Act 1 is indeed in high speed, except in v.5 where there is a repetition.

4. SETTINGS

A narrative is possible only when it happens "somewhere at some specific point of time". While point of time was discussed above as *time*, here we attempt to study about *the place* under this topic, settings. Settings can be of two types: i. Special setting ii. Chronological setting

i. Special Setting

There are two ways the implied author informs of the setting:

a. Directly: The setting is informed by the narrator or by one of the characters directly. In the words of Bar-Efrat "the narrator takes us to the site of each event showing or telling us directly what is happening there".

b. In an indirect way: This is achieved "by mentioning certain objects, actions or conditions that will immediately suggest a certain setting to the implied reader". As regards the Hagar episode, in act one there is no any setting mentioned either directly or indirectly. One has to presume from the previous passage the place where the event is happening, namely, the tent of Abraham (cf. Gen 13:3). But in act two at least two times (v. 7 and v.14) the place or setting of the encounter between the messenger and Hagar is mentioned. So we can consider that in Gen 16 the setting is mentioned directly. The settings in Gen 16:7 are therefore i. a spring and ii. Wilderness. The spring is further qualified as being on the way to Shur (v.7), being called Beer-lahai-roi (Well of the seeing alive), and located between Kadesh and Bered.

After locating the setting we need to find out the significance of the setting. According to Tolmie, to arrive at this we need to ask the following questions: Is the setting directly relevant to the rest of the narrative? Can any symbolic connotations be attached to the setting? Can a pattern of movement be detected? If so, does it have any significance?[53] Are any positive or negative feelings associated with a particular setting?[54]

ii. Chronological Setting

This is mention of the time in which a particular action happens. This is already discussed above under expressions of time. There are two places where the chronological setting is mentioned in Gen 16. a. One is in act one, the date of marriage of Hagar (v.3- giving of Hagar to Abram as wife by Sarai). It happened at the end of tenth year of Abram's dwelling in the land of Canaan. b. The second one is at the end of the episode (v.16), where the age of Abram is mentioned when Hagar gave birth Ishmael to Abram.

5. WORDS

In any narration and specially in the Biblical narration, every word is chosen with care. So every word is important in communicating the message of the text. Alter says that "the choice or the mere presence of particular single words and phrases in the biblical tale has special weight precisely because biblical narrative is so laconic"[55].

Leitwort

Unlike the modern languages where usage of different words communicating the same meaning is appreciated very much to avoid monotony, in the Biblical narratives "The repetition of single words or brief phrases often exhibits a frequency, a saliency, and a thematic significance"[56] So when a particular word or phrase is repeated again and again it has to be taken seriously. Alter has this to say, namely, "…the repetition of single words is the use of the *Leitwort*, the thematic key-word, as a way of enunciating and developing the moral, historical, psychological, or theological meanings of the story… the *Leitwort* is a principal means of punctuation."[57] The repeated word can be abstract and so point to a thematic idea, such as to see in Gen 16 or it may be concrete, like well again in the Hagar episode (Gen 16).

To emphasize again about the use of the words, Alter opines that "the fact of inclusion or exclusion of any particular lexical item itself be quite important."[58] In the Hagar story, in Gen 16:4, the choice of the word 'mistress' is very important in "She (Hagar) looked with contempt on her *mistress*". So it can be seen as a social protest of the slave against her mistress and not between two women as usually portrayed by the commentators.[59] So is also the use of the word for oppression (*ani*) - be of little account. As said above biblical author/s is/ are very careful in choosing a particular word or phrase. In other words, "There is not a great deal of narrative specification in the Bible, and so when a particular descriptive detail is mentioned... we should be alert for consequences, immediate or eventual, either in plot or theme."[60] For example the words in v.1 of Gen 16 are chosen with care and every word has a value in the story. Especially the information that Sarai was barren is going to have its consequence, so it is introduced in the first verse itself.[61] So every word in the Biblical Narrative is not without its importance.

Epithets

The Biblical narrative has lots of epithets, especially to women.[62] Alter comments on this saying, "when relational epithet is attached to a character, or, conversely, when a relational identity is stated without the character's proper name, the narrator is generally telling us something substantive without recourse to explicit commentary."[63]

The Hagar episode has lots of epithets; almost all the first 10 verses (except v.7) use epithets to mention about persons.[64] The majority of them is about the master/mistress – slave relationship. So it is enough to prove that it is a story of sociological upheaval rather than a fight between two women.

Irony

There is another way in which the words are used to give some special meaning or meanings. It is irony.

Definition: "Irony is the result of a contrast, an opposition. It can be the perception of a contrast, or a contrast between two different perceptions. The reader or the character(s) must perceive the contrast instantaneously."[65] It is embodied in an event or in an utterance of one of the characters. The character can speak in all innocence and the narrator can give it an ironic flavour.[66] For Gunn and Fewell, "when more meanings are present than the characters involved can recognize, irony is present".[67] They even define that, "Irony is incongruity of knowledge, value, or point of view. Characters think they know what they are doing when in fact they may be doing something rather different".[68] Applying this to Gen 16, by giving Hagar as wife to Abraham, Sarai thought that she was building up her very self (cf. Gen 16:2), but in fact she (Sarai) was building up Hagar. This is seen when one completes reading the episode, as God, who is at work 'behind the scene',[69] was building up Hagar. That is the irony here.

Berlin gives the definition of Uspensky, "Irony occurs when we speak from one point of view, but make an evaluation from another point of view; thus for irony the nonconcurrence of point of view on the different levels is a necessary requirement".[70]

Kinds of irony[71]

1. Verbal irony:[72] According to Gunn and Fewell, it is, "language that can be interpreted as understanding or counter stating what, on the surface, it seems to mean, also often bypasses the characters en route from narrator to reader"[73] They give the example of Judg 17:6 and 21:25 where the people were doing "what was right in their own eyes." This has to be seen as irony against the earlier incidents where 'the eyes of Yahweh' is mentioned (cf. Judg 2:11; 3:7, 12; 4:1; 6:1;10:6; 13:1). Ska gives the example of Laban and Jacob in Gen 29:19. When Laban says, "It is

better that I give her to you than that I should give her to any other man; stay with me." He did not mention which daughter he was referring, Rachel or Leah.[74]

2. Dramatic irony: This is derived from "the fact that the character knows less than the reader, or unknowingly does things which are not in his or her own best interest, or from the course of events leading to results which are the reverse of the character's aspirations".[75] In the story of selling of Joseph (Gen 37:12-36) and the story of Tamar (Gen 38), there is irony in the use of 'kid'. Judah with his brothers deceived his father by a kid (cf. Gen 37:31-33) and Tamar deceived Judah when he sent the kid (Gen 38:20-23). Thus the deceiver was deceived.[76] In 2Sam 11:11 Uriah compares his situation with that of his comrades in the battle field. But the reader will make an implicit comparison between Uriah's behavior and that of David.[77] When David says to Absalom "Go in peace" (2Sam 15:9), though he meant nothing extraordinary but Absalom's designs are not peaceful. He has planned to kill Amnon, his brother.[78] In 2 Sam 18:27 what David said as 'good tidings' is in fact the news of his son's death, a 'bad tiding' to David. In the story of Esther, "Haman is himself hung on the gallows he has prepared for Mordecai (Es 7:9-10)."[79] In the Hagar episode, in v. 2, Sarai wanted to be built up through Hagar. But in fact at the end of the story Hagar is being built up with the son and as wife of Abram while Sarai is forgotten and sidelined.[80] In all these examples "there is a contrast between the situation as perceived or hoped for by the character involved and the actual state of affairs."[81]

3. The irony of fate is a kind of dramatic irony which "highlights the connections between cause and consequence, between the individual's aspirations and what actually happens, and between character and fate".[82] Sarai had a plan to solve her problem of barrenness. But the flight of Hagar spoils Sarai's aspirations.[83] Ska gives the example of Haman who prepared a gallows for Mordecai and was hanged on it himself (cf. Esth 5:14; 7:9-10).[84]

4. Structural Irony: This means, "the writer introduces a structural feature that maintains an ironic atmosphere throughout the narration."[85] Jonah is given as an example. In the book of Jonah, everybody converts, the sailors, the Ninivites, even God changed his mind (Jon 3:10), except the prophet who preached the conversion.[86] In the story of Manoah and his wife (cf. Judg 13:1-23), it is interesting to note how the woman is intuitive at the first instant of meeting the messenger but her husband is rationalistic and doubting all thorough the narrative. This attitude of the man is mocked at in this episode.

6. DIALOGUE

In the narration there are dialogues. They have special functions especially in Biblical narratives. Two can be mentioned here:

a. Alter explains the first function of dialogue thus, "The phrase or whole sentence first stated by the narrator do not reveal their full significance until they are repeated, whether faithfully or with distortions, in direct speech by one or more of the characters".[87] In the Hagar episode for example what was narrated in vv.3-4 namely, "So, after Abram had lived ten years in the land of Canaan, Sarai, Abram's wife, took Hagar the Egyptian, her slave-girl, and gave her to her husband Abram as a wife. He went in to Hagar, and she conceived; and when she saw that she had conceived, she looked with contempt on her mistress." (Genesis 16:3-4) is repeated in v.5 in the dialogue of Sarai, i.e. "I gave my slave-girl to your embrace, and when she saw that she had conceived, she looked on me with contempt." (Gen 16:5).

Characters often repeat whole sentences or even series of sentences of each other's speech almost *verbatim*. In such cases we have to watch for the small differences that emerge in the general pattern of *verbatim* repetition. Alter explains the importance of such repetition in storytelling. According to him, "the small alterations, the reversals of order, the elaborations or deletions undergone by the statements as they are restated and sometimes restated again, will be revelations of character, moral, social, or political stance, and even plot."[88]

b. Secondly "...large part of the narrative burden is carried by dialogue, the transactions between characters typically unfolding through the words they exchange."[89] That is, when an event is important and essential the writer will try to give it through dialogue. Thus, the dialogues give a right direction to the narrative. For example, in the Bathsheba story the emphasis is more to the murder than to sexual transgression. It is clear in the dialogue of Prophet Nathan in 2Sam 12.[90]

When we come across any dialogue we have to ask some questions, such as: "Is this the first reported speech for either or both of the two interlocutors? If so, why did the writer choose this particular narrative juncture to make the character reveal himself through speech? How does the kind of speech assigned to the character – its syntax, tone, imagery, brevity or lengthiness- serve to delineate the character and his relation to the other party to the dialogue? ... we should be alert to the seeming discontinuities of biblical dialogue and ponder what they might imply."[91] So the dialogues also reveal something about the characters involved in the narration.

One more basic rule about dialogue is expressed by Gunn and Fewell and others, that is, "Characters often speak about themselves and other characters ...what characters say about themselves and about one another cannot always be relied upon since characters in biblical narrative, mimicking real life, speak to specific occasions and convey only limited human viewpoints, frequently prejudiced and self-serving".[92] So they cannot be taken as the proof of writer's viewpoint.[93] What the narrator says is to be relied while the dialogues have to be tested and decided according to the flow of the story.

The use of dialogue: According to Alter, "In the biblical story the invented dialogue is an expression of the author's imaginative grasp of his protagonists as distinctive moral and psychological figures, of their emotion-fraught human intercourse dramatically conceived; and what that entire process of imagination essentially means is the creation of fictional character."[94] According to Bar-Efrat there are two functions of dialogue: 1. "as a vehicle for the development of the plot since they do not usually convey thought and contemplation but deal rather with actions, generally focusing on the future".[95] 2. "to illuminate the human aspect, revealing such psychological features as motives and intentions, points of view and approaches, attitudes and reactions."[96]

Narration and dialogue

According to Alter "There are three general kinds of function served by the narration that is woven through or around dialogue. These are: the conveying of actions essential to the unfolding of the plot (other sorts of action are hardly ever reported) which could not be easily or adequately indicated in dialogue; the communication of data ancillary to the plot, often not strictly part of it because actions are not involved (data, in other words, essentially expository in nature); the verbatim mirroring, confirming, subverting, or focusing in narration of statement made in direct discourse by the characters"[97]

Quoting previously reported speech

Under dialogue it is also good to study about quoting of a reported speech. This can be grouped into 1. verifiable (when the original speech is present in the text) 2. non-verifiable (when the original speech is lacking). This can be further subdivided into five kinds.

Verifiable

1. We have the original speech and its exact repetition e.g. Gen 38:21-22.

2. We have the original speech and an inexact, or dissonant repetition, e.g. Gen 3:3

Non-verifiable

3. We lack the original speech because there never was one; the 'repeated' speech is a fabrication, e.g. 1Sam 19:17; 2Sam 14:7.

4. We lack the original speech because the scene in which it occurred is not narrated (although it is believable), e.g. 1Sam 24:5; 1Kings 18:10.

5. We lack the original speech even though the scene in which it should have occurred is narrated, and the speech is believable.

Conclusion

This chapter explained the subsections of Narration or the Text. This included characters, events or actions, time, settings, words and dialogue. The following chapter would discuss implied author's textual strategy.

Endnotes

[1] Cf. M. A. Powell, *What is Narrative Criticism?* London: SPCK, 1993, 35.

[2] Shimon Bar-Efrat, *Narrative Art in the Bible*, Dorothea Shefer-Vanson (Trans), Decatur: Almond Press, 1989,197.

[3] M. A. Powell, *What is Narrative Criticism?* London: SPCK, 1993, 35.

[4] Cf. J.P. Fokkelman, *Reading Biblical Narrative: An Introductory Guide*, Louisville: Westminster John Knox Press, 1999, 73.

[5] In Gen 16 except v. 4b all the other verses are in the active.

[6] V.4b (her mistress was of little account in her eyes) is in the passive.

[7] J.P. Fokkelman, *Reading Biblical Narrative: An Introductory Guide* Louisville: Westminster John Knox Press 1999, 75. (v.1 for example in Gen 16).

[8] M. A. Powell, *What is Narrative Criticism?* London: SPCK, 1993, 36.

[9] M. A. Powell, *What is Narrative Criticism?* London: SPCK, 1993, 36.

[10] R. Alter, *The Art of Biblical Narrative*. New York: Basic Books, 1981, 181.

[11] Gen 21 and 22 can be also in a way considered as parallels. Because in both Isaac is in crisis.

[12] R. Alter, *The Art of Biblical Narrative*. New York: Basic Books, 1981,181.

[13] Shimon Bar-Efrat, *Narrative Art in the Bible*, Dorothea Shefer-Vanson (Trans), Decatur: Almond Press, 1989, 142.

[14] Shimon Bar-Efrat, *Narrative Art in the Bible*, Dorothea Shefer-Vanson (Trans) Decatur: Almond Press, 1989, 142.

[15] For various discussions of time and space also cf. Shimon Bar-Efrat,*Narrative Art in the Bible*, Dorothea Shefer-Vanson (Trans) Decatur: Almond Press, 1989, 141-196.

[16] Shimon Bar-Efrat, *Narrative Art in the Bible*, Dorothea Shefer-Vanson (Trans), Decatur: Almond Press, 1989, 165.

[17] Some name it as 1. analepsis: events narrated belatedly 2. prolepsis :an event narrated prematurely.

[18] Shimon Bar-Efrat, *Narrative Art in the Bible*, Dorothea Shefer-Vanson (Trans), Decatur: Almond Press, 1989, 177.

[19] Shimon Bar-Efrat, *Narrative Art in the Bible*, Dorothea Shefer-Vanson (Trans), Decatur: Almond Press, 1989, 179.

[20] Cf. Shimon Bar-Efrat, *Narrative Art in the Bible*, Dorothea Shefer-Vanson (Trans), Decatur: Almond Press, 1989, 175-180, especially 179-180.

[21] Cf. D.F. Tolmie, *Narratology and Biblical narratives. A Practical Guide*, San Francisco: International Scholars Publications, 1999, 118, 15.

[22] Also cf. Shimon Bar-Efrat, *Narrative Art in the Bible*, Dorothea Shefer-Vanson (Trans),Decatur: Almond Press 1989, 143-144.

[23] J. L. Ska, *"Our Fathers Have Told Us" Introduction to the Analysis of Hebrew Narratives*, (SubBib 13) Rome: PIB Press, 1990, 7.

[24] Cf. D.F. Tolmie, *Narratology and Biblical narratives. A Practical Guide*, San Francisco: International Scholars Publications, 1999, 93.

[25] J. L. Ska, *"Our Fathers Have Told Us" Introduction to the Analysis of Hebrew Narratives*, (SubBib 13) Rome: PIB Press, 1990, 8.

[26] D.F. Tolmie, *Narratology and Biblical narratives. A Practical Guide*, San Francisco: International Scholars Publications, 1999,93.

[27] Cf. D.F. Tolmie, *Narratology and Biblical narratives. A Practical Guide*, San Francisco: International Scholars Publications, 1999, 93-94. Also cf. M. A. Powell, *What is Narrative Criticism?* London: SPCK, 1993, 38-39.

[28] M. A. Powell, *What is Narrative Criticism?* London: SPCK, 1993, 38-39.

[29] Cf. M. A. Powell, *What is Narrative Criticism?* London: SPCK, 1993, 38.

[30] D.F. Tolmie, *Narratology and Biblical narratives. A Practical Guide*, San Francisco: International Scholars Publications, 1999, 94. Also cf. R. Alter, *The Art of Biblical Narrative*, New York: Basic Books, 1981,63. Adele Berlin, *Poetics and Interpretation of Biblical Narrative* Winona Lake, Indiana: Eisenbrauns, 1994, 46 quotes J. Licht on scenic narrative as, "the action is broken up into a sequence of scenes. Each scene presents the happenings of a particular place and time, concentrating the attention of the audience on the deeds and the words spoken. Conflicts, direct statements of single acts, and direct speech are preeminent".

[31] Shimon Bar-Efrat, *Narrative Art in the Bible*, Dorothea Shefer-Vanson (Trans), Decatur: Almond Press 1989, 150.

[32] M. A. Powell, *What is Narrative Criticism?* London: SPCK, 1993, 38.

[33] Shimon Bar-Efrat, *Narrative Art in the Bible*, Dorothea Shefer-Vanson (Trans), Decatur: Almond Press 1989, 151.

[34] Shimon Bar-Efrat, *Narrative Art in the Bible*, Dorothea Shefer-Vanson (Trans), Decatur: Almond Press 1989, 152.

[35] The same thing can be applied to many of the miracles of Jesus. There will be lots of discourse in preparation for the miracle and the effects of it. The narrator, interestingly, will tell very little of the actual happening of the miracle (say, how in fact the water became wine or how the bread multiplied etc). Because the author is not worried about the how of the miracle as the 'modern' man/woman is curious about it (cf. Jn 2: 1-11 (miracle at Cana); Jn 6: 1:14 (multiplication of bread)).

[36] Though these words last only few minutes the whole process of convincing him would have lasted for few days.

[37] Cf. Shimon Bar-Efrat, *Narrative Art in the Bible*, Dorothea Shefer-Vanson (Trans), Decatur: Almond Press 1989, 151.

[38] Pamela Tamarkin Reis, ("Hagar Requited" *JSOT* 87 (2000), 82), points out "The use of four verbs within ten words (in Hebrew), rushes us past intercourse, through conception, realization of pregnancy and to the effect of this awareness". May be this speed according to this author (no. 21) inspired the rabbinic opinion that Hagar became pregnant after one intimacy.

[39] The act of running would have happened on one particular day but the process of reflection to flee would have lasted for few days or months.

[40] From the time of return to the time of giving birth it would have taken few months. This is what Bar-Efrat calls as "an empty period of time" (Cf. Shimon Bar-Efrat, *Narrative Art in the Bible*, Dorothea Shefer-Vanson (Trans), Decatur: Almond Press 1989, 154.) For other examples cf. 2Sam 13:23; 14:28; 1Kings 2:38-39. Here "periods of months or even years pass in the twinkling of an eye" (Shimon Bar-Efrat, *Narrative Art in the Bible*, Dorothea Shefer-Vanson (Trans), Decatur: Almond Press 1989, 154).

[41] This verse together with Gen 17:1 can be said as 'bridging time' where "time exists quantitatively but is not shaped qualitatively" Shimon Bar-Efrat, *Narrative Art in the Bible*, Dorothea Shefer-Vanson (Trans), Decatur: Almond Press, 1989, 159.

[42] Cf. D.F. Tolmie, *Narratology and Biblical narratives: A Practical Guide*, San Francisco: International Scholars Publications, 1999, 94.

[43] Cf. D.F. Tolmie, *Narratology and Biblical narratives: A Practical Guide*, San Francisco: International Scholars Publications, 1999, 94.

[44] D.F. Tolmie, *Narratology and Biblical narratives: A Practical Guide*, San Francisco: International Scholars Publications, 1999, 94.

[45] D.F. Tolmie, *Narratology and Biblical narratives: A Practical Guide*, San Francisco: International Scholars Publications, 1999, 94.

[46] Cf. D.F. Tolmie, *Narratology and Biblical narratives: A Practical Guide*, San Francisco: International Scholars Publications, 1999, 95.

[47] D.F. Tolmie, *Narratology and Biblical narratives: A Practical Guide*, San Francisco: International Scholars Publications, 1999, 100. Also cf. M. A. Powell, *What is Narrative Criticism?* London: SPCK, 1993, 39.

[48] D.F. Tolmie, *Narratology and Biblical narratives: A Practical Guide*, San Francisco: International Scholars Publications, 1999, 100. That is to say, "a one – to – one relationship exists between the events in the story level and the events in the narrative text".

[49] Cf. M. A. Powell, *What is Narrative Criticism?* London: SPCK, 1993, 39.

[50] Cf. three accounts of Paul's 'conversion' or call narrative in Acts (Cf. Acts 9:1-9; 22:4-16; 26:9-18).

[51] Shimon Bar-Efrat, *Narrative Art in the Bible*, Dorothea Shefer-Vanson (Trans) Decatur: Almond Press 1989, 160.

[52] Shimon Bar-Efrat, *Narrative Art in the Bible*, Dorothea Shefer-Vanson (Trans) Decatur: Almond Press 1989, 160-161.

[53] Desert for example is the place where humans meet God (cf. Deut 8:14f; Jer 2:6; Hos 2:16; Is 35:1; 1Kings 19:8f). In the same way well as place of annunciation (cf. Gen 16:14; 21:19) and place of one finding his/her life partner (cf. Gen 24:11; Gen 29: 1-14).

[54] Regarding the places in Bible, Bar-Efrat has this to say, " ...places in the narratives are not merely geographical facts, but are to be regarded as literary elements in which fundamental significance is embodied". (Shimon Bar-Efrat, *Narrative Art in the Bible*, Dorothea Shefer-Vanson (Trans), Decatur: Almond Press 1989, 194). Many scholars interpreted the wilderness mentioned in v.7, and its location as near to Egypt. Therefore they interpreted that Hagar was returning to her homeland, Egypt. i.e to her gods. So it is a negative interpretation of the setting. But as said above, the same wilderness can be positively interpreted as a place of encounter with the divine.

[55] R. Alter, *The Art of Biblical Narrative*, New York: Basic Books, 1981,179.

[56] R. Alter, *The Art of Biblical Narrative*, New York: Basic Books, 1981,179.

[57] R. Alter, *The Art of Biblical Narrative*, New York: Basic Books, 1981, 180.

[58] R. Alter, *The Art of Biblical Narrative*, New York: Basic Books, 1981, 180.

[59] Cf. Antony John Baptist, *Together as Sisters: Hagar and Dalit Women*, New Delhi: ISPCK, 2012, 112-113.

[60] R. Alter, *The Art of Biblical Narrative*, New York: Basic Books, 1981, 180.

[61] Cf. Antony John Baptist, *Together as Sisters: Hagar and Dalit Women*, New Delhi: ISPCK, 2012, 92-95.

[62] For example, Rahab and others are mentioned as prostitute. Are they prostitutes by profession or is it a way of identification or an attributed identity on the women by the patriarchal society? Many biblical women are mentioned only by their epithets and not by their proper name, ex. Daughter of Jephthah (Judg 11:34), the wife of Manoah (Judg 13:1-24). Interestingly the book of Ruth gives only the names of the women and not the names of husband of Naomi or the sons of Naomi or husbands of Orpha or Ruth.

[63] R. Alter, *The Art of Biblical Narrative*, New York: Basic Books, 1981, 180.Other examples are Michal (1Sam 18:20, 27, 28) and Tamar (2Sam 13).

[64] 16:1 Now *Sarai, Abram's wife*, bore him no children. She had *an Egyptian slave-girl* whose name was Hagar, 2 and Sarai said to Abram, "You see that the LORD has prevented me from bearing children; go in to *my slave-girl*, it may be that I shall obtain children by her." And Abram listened to the voice of Sarai. 3 So, after Abram had lived ten years in the land of Canaan, *Sarai, Abram's wife*, took *Hagar the Egyptian, her slave-girl*, and gave her *to her husband Abram as a wife*. 4 He went in to Hagar, and she conceived; and when she saw that she had conceived, she looked with contempt on *her mistress*. 5 Then Sarai said to Abram, "May the wrong done to me be on you! I gave my *slave-girl* to your embrace, and when she saw that she had conceived, she looked on me with contempt. May the LORD judge between you and me!" 6 But Abram said to Sarai, "*Your slave-girl* is in your power; do to her as you please." Then Sarai dealt harshly with her, and she ran away from her. 7 The angel of the LORD found her by a spring of water in the wilderness, the spring on the way to Shur. 8 And he said, "*Hagar, slave-girl of Sarai*, where have you come from and where are you going?" She said, "I am running away from *my mistress Sarai*." 9 The angel of the LORD said to her, "Return *to your mistress*, and submit to her." 10 The angel of the LORD also said to her, "I will so greatly multiply *your offspring* that they cannot be counted for multitude."

⁶⁵ J. L. Ska, *"Our Fathers Have Told Us" Introduction to the Analysis of Hebrew Narratives*, (SubBib 13) Rome: PIB Press, 1990, 57.

⁶⁶ Cf. Shimon Bar-Efrat, *Narrative Art in the Bible*, Dorothea Shefer-Vanson (Trans.), Decatur: Almond Press, 1989,

⁶⁷D.M Gunn and D.N. Fewell, *Narrative in the Hebrew Bible*, Oxford: Oxford University Press, 1993, 73.

⁶⁸ D.M Gunn and D.N. Fewell, *Narrative in the Hebrew Bible*, Oxford: Oxford University Press, 1993, 74.

⁶⁹ Cf. D.M Gunn and D.N. Fewell, *Narrative in the Hebrew Bible*, Oxford: Oxford University Press, 1993, 81.

⁷⁰ As quoted by Adele Berlin, *Poetics and Interpretation of Biblical Narrative*, Winona Lake, Indiana: Eisenbrauns, 1994,51-52. She also explains it from Gen 22:8.

⁷¹ For more explanation and examples cf. Cf. J. L. Ska, *"Our Fathers Have Told Us" Introduction to the Analysis of Hebrew Narratives*, (SubBib 13) Rome: PIB Press, 1990, 57-61.

⁷² Cf. Shimon Bar-Efrat, *Narrative Art in the Bible*, Dorothea Shefer-Vanson (Trans), Decatur: Almond Press 1989, 210.

⁷³ D.M. Gunn and D.N. Fewell, *Narrative in the Hebrew Bible*, Oxford: Oxford University Press. 1993, 74.

⁷⁴ J. L. Ska, *"Our Fathers Have Told Us" Introduction to the Analysis of Hebrew Narratives*, (SubBib 13) Rome: PIB Press, 1990, 57-58. Another example he gives is Hushai's discourse in 2Sam 16:16-17:5.

⁷⁵ Shimon Bar-Efrat, *Narrative Art in the Bible* Dorothea Shefer-Vanson (Trans.), Decatur: Almond Press, 1989, 125.

⁷⁶ Cf. R. Alter, *The Art of Biblical Narrative*, New York: Basic Books, 1981, 10-11. In the same way Jacob was asked to 'see' whether it was his son's robe or not (cf. Gen 37:32); Later, Judah was asked to see whose things are 'the signet and the cord and the staff' (cf. Gen 38:25). In both the cases the Hebrew used is הַכֶּר־נָא (haker-na).

⁷⁷ Cf. Shimon Bar-Efrat, *Narrative Art in the Bible* Dorothea Shefer-Vanson (Trans.) Decatur: Almond Press, 1989, 126-129. Also cf. 2Sam 12:5-6 where David "unknowingly passes sentence on himself when he thinks that he is condemning the rich man." (Shimon Bar-Efrat, *Narrative Art in the Bible* Dorothea Shefer-Vanson (Trans.) Decatur: Almond Press, 1989, 127.).

[78] The vow Absalom speaks of in 2 Sam 15:7-8 can be understood in two ways, "The apparent meaning is religious (an act of worship). The hidden meaning is political (Absalom decided to become king)." J. L. Ska, *"Our Fathers Have Told Us" Introduction to the Analysis of Hebrew Narratives*, (SubBib 13) Rome: PIB Press, 1990, 59.

[79] Shimon Bar-Efrat, *Narrative Art in the Bible* Dorothea Shefer-Vanson (Trans.) Decatur: Almond Press, 1989, 129.

[80] Cf. Antony John Baptist, *Together as Sisters: Hagar and Dalit Women*, New Delhi: ISPCK, 2012, 160.

[81] Shimon Bar-Efrat, *Narrative Art in the Bible* Dorothea Shefer-Vanson (Trans.) Decatur: Almond Press, 1989, 128.

[82] Shimon Bar-Efrat, *Narrative Art in the Bible* Dorothea Shefer-Vanson (Trans.) Decatur: Almond Press, 1989, 129.

[83] Cf. Antony John Baptist, *Together as Sisters: Hagar and Dalit Women*, New Delhi: ISPCK, 2012, 126-127.

[84] J. L. Ska, *"Our Fathers Have Told Us" Introduction to the Analysis of Hebrew Narratives*, (SubBib 13) Rome: PIB Press, 1990, 61.

[85] J. L. Ska, *"Our Fathers Have Told Us" Introduction to the Analysis of Hebrew Narratives*, (SubBib 13) Rome: PIB Press, 1990, 61.

[86] There are also seers who were unable to see (cf. Num 22:21-35; 1Sam 16:1-13).

[87] R. Alter, *The Art of Biblical Narrative*, New York: Basic Books, 1981, 182.

[88] R. Alter, *The Art of Biblical Narrative*, New York: Basic Books, 1981, 183.

[89] R. Alter, *The Art of Biblical Narrative*, New York: Basic Books, 1981, 182.

[90] Especially cf. "Why have you despised the word of the LORD, to do what is evil in his sight? You have struck down Uriah the Hittite with the sword, and have taken his wife to be your wife, and have killed him with the sword of the Ammonites." (2 Samuel 12:9)

[91] R. Alter, *The Art of Biblical Narrative*, New York: Basic Books, 1981, 182-183.

[92] D. M. Gunn, and D. N. Fewell, *Narrative in the Hebrew Bible*, Oxford: Oxford University Press. 1993, 68-69. Also cf. J.P. Fokkelman, *Reading Biblical Narrative: An Introductory Guide*, Louisville: Westminster John Knox Press 1999, 68.

[93] Cf. J.P. Fokkelman, *Reading Biblical Narrative: An Introductory Guide*, Louisville: Westminster John Knox Press 1999, 59.

[94] R. Alter, *The Art of Biblical Narrative*. New York: Basic Books, 1981, 36-37.

[95] Shimon Bar-Efrat, *Narrative Art in the Bible*, Dorothea Shefer-Vanson (Trans) Decatur: Almond Press 1989, 147.

[96] Shimon Bar-Efrat, *Narrative Art in the Bible*, Dorothea Shefer-Vanson (Trans) Decatur: Almond Press 1989, 147.

[97] R. Alter, *The Art of Biblical Narrative*, New York: Basic Books, 1981, 76-77.

CHAPTER - 4

The Implied
Author's Textual Strategy

The last two chapters explained the various concepts involved in the narration or reading of a text, namely, narrator, narrattee, implied author, implied reader, real author and the real reader and the various elements involved in the text such as Characters, Events/ actions, Time, Setting, words, and dialogue. This present chapter sees the text as a whole and tries to explain various strategies used by the implied author to communicate his/her ideology. This includes 1. Narrator text and character text 2. Point of View or Focalization 3. Characterization (traits) and 4. Deep structure. As we stated at the beginning of the study the implied author using the text wants to convey an ideology or an ideological perspective to the implied reader. This is called textual strategy.[1] It is presumed that, "the narrative strategy is dominated by the implied author's attempts to convey a certain ideological perspective to the implied reader".[2]

1. Narrator text and character text[3]

Fokkelman[4] divides the texts into two types. The first type is, the *main text or Narrator text*. This includes all the words used by the narrator in telling a story. The second type is the *Character text* which consists in monologue or dialogue used by any character in the text. Fokkelman continues to describe the characteristics of these two types of texts as follows.[5] The *character's text* is in present tense. It commands and expresses the characters wishes. It is worried about the imminent future. The characters are excited or dramatic. The speaker is totally committed to the matter under discussion. The *narrator's text,* on the other hand, is looking back on a distant past. The narrator changes and fine tunes his/her subject, selects the tone, overviews and orders. The narrator's text can consist of information (description), comments, explication, and value judgements. Description can include status, profession, gentile designation etc.[6]

Applying these two types of texts, we can represent Gen 16 as follows, where the Narrator texts are in italics in the text and the Character Texts are without italics.[7]

v. 1 *Now Sarai wife of Abram did not a bear child for him and she had an Egyptian maidservant and her name was Hagar.*

v. 2 *and Sarai said to Abram,* "Surely, Yahweh had shut me from giving birth to a child, I beg you, go into my maid servant, perhaps I may be built up through her". *Abram listened to the voice of Sarai.*

v. 3 *and Sarai wife of Abram took Hagar, her Egyptian maid servant at the end of the tenth year of Abram's dwelling in the land of Canaan and then she gave her to Abram her husband, for him as wife.*

v. 4 *and he went into Hagar and she conceived and (when) she saw that she had conceived, her mistress was of little account in her eyes.*

v. 5 *and Sarai said to Abram,* "The wrong done against me (is) on you, I, myself placed my maid servant in your bosom and (when) she saw that she had conceived, I am of little importance in her eyes. Let Yahweh judge between me and you".

v. 6 *and Abram said to Sarai*, " Look! Your maidservant (is) in your hand do to her the good (that is found) in your eyes". *And Sarai afflicted her and she fled from her presence.*

v. 7 *and the messenger of Yahweh found her at the spring of waters in the wilderness at the spring on the way (to) Shur.*

v. 8 *and he said*, "Hagar! Maidservant of Sarai! From where have you come? And where are you going?" *and then she replied*, "I am fleeing from the presence of Sarai my mistress"

v. 9 *and the messenger of Yahweh said to her*, "Return to your mistress and submit yourself under her hand".

v. 10 *and the messenger of Yahweh said to her*, "Indeed I will cause to multiply your offspring and it shall not be counted because of the multitude"

v. 11 *and then the messenger of Yahweh said to her*,

" Behold you (are) pregnant

and you shall give birth to a son

and you shall call his name Ishmael

for Yahweh has listened to your affliction.

v.12 But he shall be wild ass of a man,

his hand (shall be) against every one

and hand of every one (shall be) against him

and (he shall live) against all his brothers"

v.13 *and she called the name of Yahweh who spoke to her*, "You are El-roi (God of my vision)" *for she said*, "Is it even here I saw after (His) seeing me?"[8]

v.14 *that is why one called the well, Beer-lahai-roi (Well of the seeing alive). Behold (it is) between Kadesh and Bered.*

v.15. *and then Hagar gave birth to a son to Abram and then Abram called the name of his son whom Hagar gave birth, as Ishmael.*

v. 16 now Abram (was) eighty-six years when Hagar gave birth to Ishmael to Abram.

2. Point of View/Focalization

There are various perspectives from which a narrative is told. So the questions arise such as who is the character whose point of view orients the narrative perspective? Who in fact sees? Who perceives? Where is the centre of perception? Or whose perspective we are actually being given? The purpose of point of view therefore is "to understand whose telling or showing we are receiving and how these types of presentation are made".[9]

In the theatre when a drama is acted out the audience is free to look at the characters whom s/he chooses to. But in a film the viewer is restricted to see only what the camera chooses to show. In other words the director or the editor decides and allows us to see only those things which s/he wants. In the narration also the story is told to us and the implied author chooses to show only those things which s/he wants. That choice is called point of view or Focalization. So when we read a text we see through the camera eye of the narrator/ implied author. Adele Berlin points out that "The biblical narrator is omniscient in that everything is at his disposal; but he selects carefully what he will include and what he will omit. He can survey the scene from a distance, or zoom in for a detailed look at a small part of it. He can follow one character throughout, or hop from the vantage point of one to another".[10]

There are *three senses* in which the term 'point of view' can be applied: 1. Perceptual point of view: It is the perspective through which the events of the narrative are perceived; 2. Conceptual point of view: This is the perspective of attitudes, conceptions, world view; 3. Interest point of view: Here the perspective of someone's benefit or disadvantage is narrated.[11] Perception and conception generally refer to the person doing the seeing, i.e., the subject of the action, while interest refers to the person being seen i.e., the object.

In Gen 16, though the perspective of Hagar is not directly given, the *interest point of view* is around her. That is to say, the whole narrative speaks of her interest[12] and the reader is interested to know what will happen of Hagar than to Sarai. Hagar's presence is assumed in all the scenes and she reacts in act I and acts in act II. So we can say of Hagar, what Berlin says of Ruth, that Hagar is the heroine, though she is not the main character.

Berlin lists *three types of point of view*: 1. The camera stays on one character for most of the story (cf. Gen 22) 2. The Camera remains stationary as characters come and go 3. The Camera is to jump from one scene to another independently of characters (cf. 2Sam 18:19-32).[13] The presentation of many points of view gives the narrative depth and makes it a good narrative. But in a short narrative as Gen 16 we cannot expect many points of view. In Gen 16 camera remains stationary in act I and follows Hagar in Act II.

Study of specific words, phrasing, and syntactic arrangements will help the reader to find out the point of view. Accordingly there are *different levels of Point of View*.[14] 1. The ideological level: "This refers to the point of view according to which the events of the narrative are evaluated or judged – i.e., where certain actions (are) approved or disapproved".[15] 2. The phraseological levels: The linguistic features in the discourse decide this. 3. The spatial and temporal levels: It is nothing but *the ways of camera view* explained above. 4. The Psychological level: It involves *the external and internal* points of view. The Point of View is said to be *internal* when there is the internal analysis of events when the main character tells his or her own story or when an omniscient narrator tells about internal thoughts or feelings of a character. The Point of View is said to be *external* when there is an outside observation of events.

The Locus of focalization of Gen 16 is *external focalization*.[16] The events are narrated in such a way that they are perceived by an onlooker who does not play any role in the story.[17] One can detect also *internal focalization* in Gen 16.[18] In vv. 1-6 it can be argued that it is perceived through the eyes of Sarai. Especially, one may refer to Gen 16:2 "You see that the LORD has prevented me from bearing children; go in to my slave-girl; it may be that I shall obtain children by her." and Gen 16:5 "May the wrong done to me be on you! I gave my slave-girl to your embrace, and when she saw that she had conceived, she looked on me with contempt. May the LORD judge between you and me!" One can see also internal focalization from the point of Hagar. Her inner feeling, knowledge and thoughts are expressed in Gen 16:4. The knowledge of Hagar is expressed in the words as "she saw that she had conceived" and her inner feeling in "her mistress was of little account in her eyes". In Gen 16:13 the speech of Hagar expresses the inner feeling of wonder and surprise. So the first part of Gen 16 gives the Point of View of Sarai and Hagar.

The movement between the focalized objects is also important to find out the emphasis and the focalization of the author. In 1Sam 1:9-18 the movement is between Hannah and Eli.[19] The movement between 'the focalized objects' in Gen 16 is as follows. In vv.1-6 Sarai initiates most of the actions and others only react to it. In vv.7-12 the messenger of Yahweh is the main character who speaks. In v.13 however Hagar is alone and she is focalised.

Ways of finding out the Point of View/ Focalization

After explaining what point of view means and showing its various senses, types and levels, it still remains unclear on how to find out a point of view. For this we summarize some of the ways that are presented by Adele Berlin.[20]

i. Naming

Most of the characters have names but they are also referred to with some other words such as brother, father, son, etc., So, "the use of these relationship terms is an important sign of significant relationships within the story"[21] and way of viewing the characters and an indicator of point of view.

In Gen 16 three characters in the story refer to Hagar as "maid servant": Sarai (Gen 16:2, 5), Abram (v.6) and the messenger of Yahweh (v.8).[22] Interestingly the narrator (v.1) and the messenger call her with her proper name and also her status as maidservant (for the narrator (in v. 1) the status comes first and the proper name but for the messenger (in v. 8) the name comes first and then the social status).[23] Sarai and Abram never call Hagar by her proper name. They never address her directly. She is only *spoken of* and *not spoken to*. Sarai and Hagar never appear together. For Sarai and Abram she is only a functional entity and not a person. They represent the social status of Hagar.[24] Interestingly Hagar who has 'liberated' herself from Sarai also identifies Sarai as 'her mistress' (Gen 16:8). Hagar uses this word, as in Gen 16:4, to identify the struggle between Sarai, the mistress and Hagar, the maid-servant. So it is a social revolt and not a personal quarrel between the two women. So here at least three points of view are expressed, that of the a. author and messenger, b. Sarai and Abram, and c. Hagar.

ii. Inner life expressed in verbs of perception

Another method of presenting the point of view is "by informing the reader what he thought, felt, feared, etc., - in other words, by portraying the inner life of the character... how the character perceives the events of the story".[25] This is communicated through the verbs of perception such as 'to see'. In Gen 16 the verb 'to see' is used to express the point of view of Hagar in v. 4 (when she *saw* that she had conceived, she looked with contempt on her mistress.) and in v. 13 ("Have *I really seen God* and remained alive after *seeing him?*") and the point of view of Sarai in v. 5 (when she *saw* that she had conceived, *she looked* on me with contempt).[26]

iii. The term *hinneh*

Hinneh is a small particle in Hebrew language with lots of meaning and uses.[27] In general, as McCarthy observes, "There is an emotional overtone when it is used. The user is moved about the connection, not neutral toward it, and the connective colors the thing connected... In all this the expression remains exclamatory with an emotional note".[28] So it is not only the meaning[29] but also the emotion that is important in understanding the meaning of *hinneh*. Exegesis should try to get both. McCarthy even goes to say *Wᵉhinnẹh* "usually carries an overtone of feeling".[30]

On the use of *wehinneh* Ska has this to say, "Often (but not always) this particle indicates a shift from the omniscient narrator's point of view to the perspective of one of the characters"[31]. The function of this word according to Berlin[32] is 1. "attention-getter".[33] In the direct discourses, "It helps the hearer to zero in on a particular person or event".[34] 2. an indicator of point of view. According to Bar-Efrat,

"In these cases the narrator explicitly informs us that what is being described is what one of the characters is seeing at that moment".[35] 3. a time reference; as such it can mark suddenness[36]. 4. a quick succession of events with little or no lapse of time. 5. the introduction of a new figure into a scene after the scene has been set by previous narration.

The use of 'behold' (*hinneh*) in Gen 16:

wehinneh is used in Gen 16 four times:

i. It is used in v.2 where it is the perspective of Sarai, of her barrenness (either she acknowledges that God is the cause of her barrenness or she blames God for the same) and proposal to use Hagar for her (Sarai's) advantage. She sees Hagar only as "maidservant" and not as a person. She does not use Hagar's proper name anywhere. It is the perspective of Sarai, one of oppression and exploitation.[37]

ii. In v.6, where it is used for the second time, it is found in the words of Abram. Therefore, it expresses his perspective. It confirms and justifies the oppression of Hagar by Sarai.

iii. In contrast to these two point of views, there is another (third) use of *hinneh* in v.11. It is used in contrast to the previous two occasions. While the first two are against Hagar this one is supportive and sympathetic to Hagar. In the third one it is about the fact that Hagar is pregnant. And it is the point of view of the messenger of Yahweh (or Yahweh Himself) so it has to be accepted and cannot be refuted.[38]

iv. The last time where *wehinneh* is used (Gen 16:14) does not express perspective of any character in the narrative but on the identification of place where Hagar had the theophany and epiphany.[39] The place stands for liberation and hope. So v.14

stands in contrast to vv.2 and 6. While the first two uses of *hinneh* stand for the oppression, the latter two uses of *hinneh* stand for liberation and subjecthood of Hagar.

iv. Circumstantial Clauses

They can also indicate point of view even when the verb of perception and *hinneh* are absent.[40]

v. Direct discourses and Narration

Direct discourse is "the most dramatic way of conveying the character's internal psychological and ideological points of view".[41] The discourse of Sarai in Gen 16:2 may be presenting her ideological point of view about her barrenness. We may also have to compare the direct discourse and the related narration of the same. If there are verbal similarities it means that the narrator is confirming the words of the character.[42]

vi. Alternative Expressions

Sometimes the narrator uses synonyms of one word and accordingly the point of view of the character changes. For example see 2Sam 6 where different words used for the word 'to dance' by different characters and accordingly their point of view changes.

It is the richness of the text/ narration when the narrator "combines these individual points of view into a unified presentation".[43] When many perspectives are presented, Berlin says, "there is no clear right and wrong. Each character's actions are justified from his point of view".[44] That means "every one of the point of view in a text makes claims to be the truth and struggles to assert itself in the conflict with opposing ones".[45] In the words of Berlin, "conflicting viewpoints may vie for validity".[46] The role of the reader is active where he/she should try to understand it and at the end he/she should establish his/her own point of view. It is also possible in multiple points of view, as in Esther, "the characters are unaware of each other's point of view. The reader has the benefit of knowing both views, and therefore his point of view differs from that of the characters. This allows the reader to comprehend how the misunderstanding occurred, and enjoy the comedy of it."[47] But in the Biblical narrative it has always to be kept in mind that the Point of View of God, or His messenger[48] is to be taken seriously and accepted without raising question. Thus all the words of the messenger of God in Gen 16 are to be considered positively. Divine voice from heaven is also reliable point of view (cf. Mk 1:11).

3. Characterization[49]

For Tolmie, "Character can be regarded as the spice of narrative".[50] Character or characterization refer to the way persons are presented in the story. According to Powell's definition "Characters are the actors in a story, the ones who carry out the various activities that comprise the plot... constructs of the implied author, created to fulfill a particular role in the story".[51] Therefore characterization is "the process through which the implied author provides the implied reader with what is necessary to reconstruct a character from the narrative".[52] According to Boris Uspensky characterization takes place in four planes: 1. Spatial-temporal plane – referring to actions, 2. phraseological plane – referring to speech, 3. the psychological plane – referring to thoughts and 4. the ideological plane referring to beliefs and values.

Some Presuppositions/Assumptions in Characterization:
The present day reader, who is accustomed to documentation and historical accuracy of the report of any event, has to be cautioned of some presuppositions that are involved in characterization. These are very important especially when there are some readers who think that Bible reports everything as it happened. We have to keep in mind that, in the Bible the events and history are given in literary form.

1. What characterisation is not: "It is not a study of details of their psychology nor a verification of whether they are realistic or not".[53] In words of Bar- Efrat, "it makes no difference whether the characters are imaginary or whether they actually existed".[54] In the words of Adele Berlin, "we should not confuse a historical individual with his narrative representation".[55] In other words what we have in the text is a representation of reality which does not correspond in every detail to reality. Many a time we are tempted "to take as real that which is only a representation of reality".[56]

2. We know the characters *only as they are presented* in the narratives. We have no way of veryfying how they were in real life or in other words how accurate the Bible narrates the historical person.

3. Unlike in other literatures "In many biblical narratives a person's character is not regarded as constant, but as something continually shifting and changing".[57] A reader who is accostumed to see characters like Abram and Sarai in a positive way as father of faith and as matrirach should be prepared to see them in some other way in Gen 16. May be they are presented differently in other passages but here they are presented in a little bit of a negative way. So

the characters are not stable.[58] There is one thing special to biblical characters, that is, "The Bible, as is well-known, does not obscure its heroes' weaknesses, and so even such characters as Abraham, Moses and David are depicted not as ideal people but as human beings with both good and bad in them."[59]

Some Ways of Characterization

It is very difficult to point out in one word or sentence how characterization is done. According to Alter, "Character can be revealed through the report of actions; through appearance, gestures, postures, costume; through one character's comments on another; through direct speech by the character; through inward speech, either summarized or quoted as interior monologue; or through statements by the narrator about the attitudes and intentions of the personages, which may come either as flat assertions or motivated explanations."[60] Here we make an attempt to list out some of the ways how characterization is done.

A. Evaluative point of view

This is of two types: (a) Evaluative point of view of implied author. This means "general perspective that an implied author establishes as normative for a work".[61] According to Powell there can be also (b) evaluative point of view of a particular character. That is "the norms, values, and general worldview that govern the way a character looks at things and renders judgments upon them".[62] So one can have an evaluative point of view of the implied author and that of Hagar.

B. Character traits

A trait is "any relatively stable or abiding personal quality associated with a character"[63] Powell defines it as "any distinguishable, relatively enduring way in which one individual differs from another"[64] That is to say, any persistent personal quality can be named as a trait. They are not most of the time said directly. They are to be inferred from the text. The traits are found basing on direct characterisation and indirect characterisation.

B.i. Direct Characterization

Bar-Efrat calls direct characterization as "the direct shaping of the characters"[65] which includes 1. Outward Appearance: Very little of physical appearance is said in Biblical narratives. If at all it is given, it is given for the "advancing the plot or explaining its course"[66] 2. Inner personality: There are two kinds of direct statement i. character traits or moral traits ii. mental states.

The Direct Characterisation can be broadly divided into three groups. The first group is characterization *voiced by God*. This according to Bar – Efrat has absolute validity even more than that of the narrator.[67] The second group is *by human beings*. The character can be mentioned by the narrator directly or by any character in the narrative. If it is mentioned by the narrator it is to be accepted without question. But if it is mentioned by any character in the narration it is to be tested with other texts and accepted or denied.[68]

Applying these two to hagar episode, in Gen 16:12 the narration about the character of Ishmael can be said to be the character *mentioned by God*. The character of Hagar, (basing only on the passages of the narrator), is *mentioned by the narrator* in the following instances: Hagar[69] (v.1); Egyptian, Maidservant, as wife (v.3); she (Hagar) saw that she had conceived and that her mistress was of little account in her eyes (v.4); Sarai afflicted her and she fled from her presence (v.6); she (Hagar) called the name of Yahweh who spoke to her (v.13); Hagar gave birth to a son to Abram (vv.15 and 16). So the following traits of Hagar can be listed: 1.Egyptian(2x), 2. maid servant (2x), 3. wife (1x directly, 3x (vv.15-16) implicitly), 4. her knowledge as one conceived, 5. her self-assertion in front of her mistress, 6. as one who was afflicted, 7. as one who flees from oppression, 8. as one who names God, 9. as one coming back and affirming her right and that of her child. One may criticize that these are derived from the narration (of course from the part where the narrator speaks) but nowhere the narrator directly mentions the character of Hagar. Ska would call it as "direct narrative statement".[70]

The third group is, the traits *mentioned by the characters in the text or by one of the participants of an action*: There are some traits that are mentioned by the characters in the narrative itself. This "sheds light on both the person judged and the one making the judgment, while at the same time enabling the former to react (either by word or by deed) and thus to reveal still more."[71] In the Hagar episode the characterization of Hagar is done by characters in the narrative itself such as Sarai, Abram, the messenger of Yahweh and Hagar herself.

a. According to Sarai: "my maid servant" (vv. 2 and 5): we can accept it as characterisation of Hagar because the narrator also mentions it; "she saw that she had conceived, I am of little importance in her eyes" (v. 5): These two statements are accepted because they are also mentioned by the narrator in v.4.

b. According to Abram: "your maid servant ..."(v. 6): This can also be accepted because as mentioned above the narrator also says the same thing in vv. 1 and 3; "do to her the good (that is found) in your eyes" (v.6): Though it speaks of Hagar it does not speak about the traits/character of Hagar. She is only recipient of the action. Abram grants his sanctions for the oppression.

c. According to the messenger of Yahweh: "Hagar! Maidservant of Sarai!" (v. 8): both can be accepted since the narrator also says both in vv. 1 and 3; Though it is startling to hear the words 'maid servant' from the messenger, he has not said anything bad about the character of Hagar. He said what the author has already said two times. According to our understanding of characterization – whatever the narrator says about the character is accepted as trait. So we accept the fact of Hagar being maid servant as her trait. The messenger, however, uses the proper name of Hagar. He/ She is the only character in the episode who addresses Hagar directly, using her proper name. So he considers her as a person with her subjecthood. He also uses the word 'maid servant'. He uses it, however, not in a derogative sense but in the sense of social identity, that is, the way in which society continues to see her. Even Hagar will see herself in that way in v.8 when she says, "I am fleeing from the presence of Sarai my mistress". After she had fled from Sarai the title 'maid servant' is no more an indication of oppression but only a social identity.

d. According to Hagar herself: "I am fleeing from the presence of Sarai my mistress" (v. 8): This can be accepted because the narrator had already said it in v. 6. Here we should note that she does not say directly that she is the maidservant of Sarai but she only says it implicitly what the narrator (vv.

1, 3), Sarai (vv.2, 5), Abram (v.6) and the messenger (v.8) have said. Therefore almost all the characters call her maidservant. So implicitly she refers herself as maid servant by referring to Sarai her mistress. But as mentioned above after she had fled from Sarai, these titles (mistress, maid servant) are only for social identification and not indication of oppression and still less acceptance and justification of oppression which they originally denoted. On the contrary, basing on vv. 15-16 we can say what really remains at the end in the view point of the narrator is 1. the name of Hagar (used three times), i.e her personhood or subjecthood 2. the fact that she gave birth to a son (used three times), i.e her motherhood. The personhood (subjecthood) and motherhood are the two characteristic traits that are proper to Hagar according to the narrator. All the rest are socially constructed traits and imposed on her by the patriarchal (Abram) and oppressive (Sarai-mistress) structures.

Here we cannot make a list of the character traits of Hagar according to different characters of the narration. Because, everyone holds them differently according to his/her vantage point of view. This makes the narrative rich and involves the reader to find out the fitting character traits of Hagar.

Critic of the use of direct characterization: Strictly speaking direct characterization is a specific trait that is "mentioned directly, for example, by means of an adjective (He was a good man), an abstract noun (God is love) or another noun (she is a woman)".[72] So applying this definition, only the following traits can be said of Hagar according to direct characterization: Egyptian, maid servant, wife, her name (personhood).

B.ii.   Indirect Characterization

Here "a given trait is not named, but portrayed or illustrated. The implied reader has to consider the information provided and formulate it in terms of a trait".[73] The biblical narrative contains more indirect characterization than direct. To find out traits of indirect characterisation one can proceed in two ways: i. By studying the actions of the character ii. By studying the speeches of the character.[74] According to Bar –Efrat, "the reader has to interpret these details and construct the character's mental and emotional make-up".[75] So the reader has to do mental efforts and increase his/ her participation.

i.   The actions of a character

For Bar-Efrat when we study the action of the character, "we have to build hypotheses about people's motives. These hypotheses will be based on our knowledge of other actions and things said by the same person, as well as on our understanding of human psychology".[76]

The actions involved in Gen 16 and the hypotheses that can be built:

1. "she (Hagar) conceived" (v.4): Externally it seems as if this is not something special or great. But given the context and the fact of barrenness of Sarai (v.1) this speaks of fertility and youthfulness of Hagar. She had no difficulty in conceiving as against her mistress and matriarch.

2. "she (Hagar) saw that she had conceived" (v.4): This informs of Hagar's awareness of her new status as a mother to a child of Abram, the patriarch. She is aware of her rights and privileges as wife and mother. She realized her personhood and subjecthood. This is the moment of her self-realization. This is an action without words (as v.6).

3. "her mistress was of little account in her eyes" (v. 4): Here there is a problem on how to understand this sentence. Whose action is this, Sarai's or Hagar's? Therefore there are two ways of seeing it.

In the perception of Sarai, it would mean of Sarai's thinking that she had become little in the eyes of Hagar. Grammatically speaking, Sarai is the grammatical subject of the sentence. Sarai, who wanted Hagar to conceive a child for her is not happy about this new situation. The emphasis shifts from the need of a child to being great in the eyes of the maidservant. Sarai is not willing to sacrifice her social status for the sake of the child. Strictly speaking, the text does not speak of any disrespect, ill-treatment, retaliation, revolution or revolt of Hagar. Hagar did not speak or act in such a way to appropriate her right. She only conceived and became aware of the fact that she has conceived. This has produced a fear, littleness, threat in Sarai and she imagined as if she has become little in the eyes of Hagar.

The action can also be studied as if it is of Hagar's or as Hagar did some actions that provoked Sarai.[77] We can hold that Hagar asserted her right.[78] If so, then it is the action of Hagar, an important action that turned the direction of the whole story. This action of Hagar upset Sarai and her whole program. So Hagar upsets the social order. She asserted her right as wife and mother. She became aware of her personhood and subjecthood and affirmed it. We should also note that the character's actions also include "those acts that could or should have been performed".[79]

We cannot but enjoy the beautiful way through which the narrator had brought the whole thing, the crucial and controversial act. Given the rigid hierarchical and patriarchal system of his/her time he/she could not openly report and narrate the revolutionary acts of Hagar. But at the same time he/she brings it out using the eyes, perception of Sarai. The gravity is brought out not directly but indirectly through how Sarai perceives it. Sarai goes to the extent of considering Abram as her opponent and antagonist against whom God has to judge.[80]

This brings about Hagar's trait as i. One who did not confine or did not accept the hierarchical social order, ii. One who did not allow herself to be used, exploited for some one's benefits, profit and advantage, iii. One who stood against oppression and iv. One who asserted her subjecthood and personhood, asserted her rights and privileges.

4. "she (Hagar) fled from her presence" (v. 6): When her mistress and the husband are against her, when the former oppresses her and the latter sanctions it, Hagar on her part is not willing to suffer silently for nothing. She executes the only option that is left to her, for that matter anybody who is in her situation, that is to flee from oppression. So the characteristic traits of Hagar here are i. that she is not willing to suffer unjustly and for no reason or benefit, ii. that she who acts taking the ground realities of her life situation. This is an example of action without words.

5. "and *then she replied*, "I am fleeing from the presence[81] of Sarai my mistress" (v. 8): This is the encounter with God (messenger of Yahweh) and she speaks for the first time in the whole narrative. Her personhood was recognized by the messenger. She is called by her proper name. She is addressed to or talked to for the first time. Earlier Sarai and Abram spoke about her and never to her. To

the messenger who recognized her personhood she also speaks as a person. So the trait of person-to-person relationship is seen here. As Fokkelman points out, "The most important window on the character's emotional and conceptual perspectives is their own words, at least if they are not deceiving us or their conversation partner".[82] If so this is the main window with which we can come to know the emotional and conceptual perspective of Hagar about her own situation.

6. and *she called the name of Yahweh* who spoke to her, "You are El-roi (God of my vision)" *for she said*, "Is it even here I saw after (His) seeing me?" (v. 13):[83] Hagar becomes aware of the fact that she had an encounter with God, that she had theophany and epiphany, that she had seen God and that she is alive even after this encounter. Because of this encounter she got meaning for her life, vision for the future, a strategy and plan to overcome, a hope for the future. So the trait is that she is a mystic and theologian who could articulate her God-experience. She had articulated that experience in clear and sensible terms.[84] She dares to give a name to God who appeared to her and called Him with a name. She is the first and only person in the biblical history who gave a name to God calling God in the second person, "you".[85]

7. "and then *Hagar gave birth to a son to Abram* and then Abram called the name of his son whom Hagar gave birth, as Ishmael. Now Abram (was) eighty-six years when Hagar gave birth to Ishmael to Abram." (v. 15-16): The information that Hagar gave birth to a son to Abram is repeated three times in these two verses. Though it is the natural consequence of v.4, the situation is not the same

as that of v.4. In fact, it is the reversal of vv. 1-4. Now there is no mention of Sarai. Hagar gives birth to a son to Abram and not to Sarai as Sarai wanted. In v.2 Sarai wanted to be built up through Hagar and a child that will be born from her. But on the contrary, Hagar is built up as wife and mother. Ishmael is born in the house of Abram and named by him. So he is the first son of Abram and Abram himself recognizes it by giving him name. So Ishmael and implicitly Hagar have their right and privilege in the house of Abram as son and as wife and mother.

b. Character's speech

As quoted already, according to Fokkelman, "the most important window on the character's emotional and conceptual perspectives is their own words, at least if they are not deceiving us or their conversation partner".[86] In the opinion of Bar-Efrat, "all speech reflects and exposes the speaker, while it sometimes also brings to light qualities of the person being addressed (or reveals the speaker's opinion of that person)".[87] So any speech or dialogue of a particular character in the narrative is to be studied carefully.

In Gen 16 Hagar speaks two times (v. 8 and 13) and she is deceiving neither the reader nor the conversing partner. So her dialogue can reveal her character traits and her emotional and conceptual perspective.

1. "and then she replied, "*I am fleeing from the presence of Sarai my mistress*" (v. 8):

Here we have to read the real pain and agony of Hagar who suffered oppression. She had no other option but to flee from Abram's tent.[88] The words of Hagar do not contain any polite or formal address[89] as it is found in the speech of the messenger. She is speaking directly about the crude reality of life, as can be seen in the words of Joab in 2Sam 19:5-7 and that of Nathan in 2Sam 12:1-14. Hagar, without polished words or refinement, expresses her situation i.e., as one fleeing from oppression and her inferior social status.[90] This deviation from the accepted style of addressing to the stranger, much more to the messenger of Yahweh, adds weight to the characterization of Hagar.

The messenger asks two questions to her, one is relating to her past and another relating to her future. But Hagar replies only to the first and not to the second. She is aware of her past and her history. The words "I am fleeing" implicitly brings forth the amount of humiliation, suffering and oppression that she suffered in the tent of Abram under Sarai and Abram. So she knew of her past and her suffering. She does not answer to the second question namely, "And where are you going?" She is not aware of the future. She did not think of the future. She did not have any plan or strategy for the future. All that she knew was that she was suffering and she has to get away from it. So the characteristic trait of Hagar here is that she had no knowledge of future, no plan or strategy for the future or to win the battle. All she now needs is an external help, force, guide to suggest plan and to win the struggle.[91] As Tolmie points out, "the style of speech may be indicative of a certain social class, profession or dwelling place"[92] Here these words of Hagar directly indicate the social class of Sarai (i.e., mistress) and implicitly her own (i.e., maidservent).

2. And she called the name of Yahweh who spoke to her, "*You are El-roi* (God of my vision) " for she said, "*Is it even here I saw after (His) seeing me?*" (v. 13):

According to Bar-Efrat, "speech which is intended solely to express emotions and is not addressed to anyone is rare".[93] But this verse contains such kind of speech where Hagar in the height of her religious experience expresses her emotions. Her speech is not addressed to any human person but to Yahweh. So a character trait emerging from this saying of Hagar is that she articulates her religious experience in clear terms.

On the whole, Hagar speaks two times in the episode. When she speaks for the first time she speaks of her plight (flight from the house of Abram because of the oppression, v.8). When she speaks for the second time, she speaks of her dignity, worth and liberation (v.13). This is completely in contrast to Act one where she never speaks, is never spoken to but only spoken of (vv.2, 5-6). So from one spoken of Hagar turns out to be the one spoken to and finally as one who speaks. This, in a way, is the journey of her liberation.

C. Environment

The physical surroundings in which a character is portrayed may also indicate certain traits of the character.[94] There are two environments depicted in Gen 16, the spring of water and wilderness. i. the spring of waters or well: It is a sign of hope in the biblical tradition.[95] So the second part of our episode begins with a note of hope and also the presence of the well reiterated at the end. ii. Wilderness is a sign of desperateness[96] and a place of encounter with the divine.[97] Putting the mention of these two places together we can say that a characteristic trait that is depicted here is one of hope among the situation of forsakenness, desperation, isolation and suffering alone.

D. Name of the Character

Ska briefs the importance of a name in the Biblical world thus, "A very common way to "characterize" a personage is to give him or her a name... the name indicates more than one quality or a constellation of qualities".[98] It also has anticipatory function in the stories. The name of Hagar means 'sojourn'.

E. Character's Inner Life

There are various ways through which the inner life of the character is expressed: 1. "direct description" or "direct narrative statement" by the narrator.[99] Biblical narrators directly disclose the inner motives, intentions or states of mind of the characters.[100] 2. Interior monologue: Such is rare in Biblical texts, but Gen 16:13 can be grouped as interior monologue.[101] 3. Dramatization of inner life and character through dialogue.[102] This can be done in three ways. A. "Bible frequently introduces a new or a secondary character onto the stage in order to the dramatize the inner state of the hero"[103] This however is not found in Gen 16. B. In some cases, we find a confidant or a counsellor.[104] C. The revealing dialogue between husband and wife.[105] This can be applied to Gen 16 where Abram and Sarai speak.[106] 4. Ska speaks of yet another way of expressing the inner life of a character. For him, "expression of inner life is found mostly in lyric texts... it is interesting to notice that the Biblical narratives often shift to poetry when they want to express strong feelings."[107]

F. Intervention of Divinities, Visions, Oracles, Dreams and Supernatural Forces.

Here we need to note at least three points:

1. The very fact that God decides to appear to someone or sends His messenger to someone means that this person

is shown as the "protagonist" of the narrative. In Gen 16 God's messenger searches and finds Hagar and speaks to her. So she is the protagonist (heroine). God did not appear to Abram or to Sarai in this episode.

2. God does not intervene in the events often. The narrator reserves the theophany only to important persons and at the crucial point of the story or history. In the words of Ska, "God's interventions are normally decisive and often occur when the narrative reaches a dead lock or comes to the 'cross-roads'".[108] In the episode of Gen 16 also it is a crucial point in which God's messenger intervenes. The plan of Sarai is distorted and she remains barren. There is no way of proceeding further and realising the promise of the son to Abram. Also from the point of view of Hagar it is crucial. What is she about to do? Where she is heading for? What will happen to her, a lone slave, pregnant women at that and to the innocent child in her womb? At this crucial point God intervenes.

3. With the intervention of God or His messenger the stand of the reader changes dramatically. Ska explains it saying, "The empathy of the reader depends very much on God's intervention... These characters acquire more depth and invite the reader to empathize with them in their predicament mostly because God speaks to them".[109] This fits perfectly well to Hagar episode both in Gen 16 and Gen 21. Any reader of Gen 16, at the beginning of the story, especially at v.4, will not be happy or approve of what Hagar has done. They would say that Hagar had betrayed her mistress. But when the messenger of God searches her and speaks to her, slowly the mentality of the reader changes in favour of Hagar.[110]

G. Minor Characters

In the view of Bar-Efrat minor characters are also one of the factor that reveals the character in an indirect way.[111] It is at times difficult to distinguish between the main and minor characters in a narrative. A character who is secondary in one episode will be main character in an another episode. Hagar for example is a minor character in Gen but a main character in Gen 16. So here for us Abram and Sarai become minor characters. Regarding the contribution of the minor characters to the main character Bar-Efrat says, "the positive or negative parallel between the primary and secondary characters is not enough to shape the characters, but it provides emphasis and colour. The minor characters serve as a background against which the personalities of the main ones stand out."[112] In our episode the character of Hagar is positively enhanced through the negative (Sarai) or 'neutral' (Abram) behaviours of the minor characters like Sarai and Abram.[113]

Summary of Traits of Hagar's Character[114]

There are different traits of Hagar's character that are explicit in Gen 16. Let me mention a few of them. The first trait that is revealed in v. 1 is that "Hagar the Egyptian is single, poor and bonded; she is also young and fertile."[115] In v. 4, by asserting her right as wife of Abraham and mother of 'first born' of Abraham, the trait that is revealed is that she claimed her subjecthood and self-worth. In v. 6 the trait of Hagar is as one who suffered more severely under Sarai. It is an attempt to wipe out Hagar.[116] The searching and finding of Hagar by the messenger of God attest the character of Hagar as one who deserves positive consideration. Thus she is worth of dignity and equality.[117]As the story concludes (in vv. 15-16) the social position of Hagar is completely changed as compared to her situation in vv.1, 3, 6.[118] So the character traits of Hagar comprise both suffering as foreign slave girl and self-assertion for liberation and subjecthood.

Classification of the Character of Hagar

After a long discussion about some of the aspects of characterization, here let us try to classify the character of Hagar according to the theories of various authors.[119] Some authors tend to classify characters as *major and minor* depending upon the proportion of the space they occupy in the text. We must also admit that such distinction is a "matter of the reader's perspective."[120] Gunn and Fewell give the example from the book of Esther, "male commentators argue for the primacy of Mordecai while female commentators argue for the primacy of Esther".[121] In the same way, Hagar for example is a minor character for many commentators but here we study Hagar as major character (at least in Gen 16).[122] With this understanding here we present some of the theories of the authors on the type of characters and apply them to Hagar.

i.   Flat and Round Characters

E.M. Forster classifies the characters into *flat character and round character*. In case of flat characters, "we know only the surface of the person. Such characters are introduced briefly and we will never know anything more about them. Often these personalities are summarized by a single trait".[123] According to Powell their "traits are all consistent and predictable".[124] For Gunn and Fewell flat character, "possesses few qualities or personality traits (perhaps only one) and, hence, is often rather predictable".[125] The round characters on the other hand, "have more depth and their personality often contains conflicting even contradictory tendencies".[126] According to Gunn and

Fewell, "round characters exhibit a conglomeration of traits, many of which are even contradictory. Such diversity and inconsistency may convey realism... they have the capacity to grow, to develop, to change their minds, to surprise the reader as well as the other characters in the story ... they, like the real people in our lives, are elusive, always evading complete definition or explanation".[127] Hagar of Gen 16 can be grouped as round character.[128] She touches both the extremes, a docile, obedient, unassuming maidservant in vv. 1-3, on the one hand but an assertive and fleeing Hagar on the other hand. She "is capable of surprising the reader in a convincing way"[129] as D. F. Tolmie puts it. We list the following reasons to say that Hagar surprises the reader: She dared to look down on her mistress and she dared to assert her right. She was courageous enough to flee from her mistress, from her oppression and oppressors. The appearance of God and the promise given to Hagar, as that of Abram is surprising. A foreign, maid servant is promised a multitude of descendent by Yahweh God. Hagar seeing God face to face and living afterwards is also surprising. Above all Hagar gives a name to God which is unimaginable in the Yahwistic religion.

ii. Full-fledged, Type and Agent

Adele Berlin divides the character types into three, i. A full-fledged character which is like round character. These characters "are much more complex, manifesting a multitude of traits, and appearing as 'real people'".[130] ii. A type, which can be equalized with a flat character iii. An agent, who is a functionary[131] and "about whom nothing is known except what is necessary for the plot".[132] About Biblical narratives she says, "the same person may appear as a full fledged character in one story and as a type or agent in another".[133] Applying this to the character of Hagar we can come to the following conclusions.

The character of Hagar *in the whole book of Genesis* can be said to be an agent. She is not the main character in this book. The patriarchs are the main characters. As Bathsheba is depicted as agent in 2 Sam 11-12,[134] Hagar is an agent in the Abraham cycle to slow down the suspense[135] of the fulfilment of the promise of a son to Abram and she is driven out of the main story together with her son when a son is born to Sarai (cf. Gen 21). The implied author does not use the character of Hagar more than for what is needed for the general plot of the story.[136]

When we consider the episode *in Gen 16 alone,* we can very well say that Hagar is a full-fledged character (round character). The following reasons can be added to the above ones.[137] Hagar is introduced as a foreigner (Egyptian), low in social status (maidservant), used as surrogate, elevated to be a wife, she affirms her subjecthood, revolts, tries to upset the existing social order and tries to reverse it. She is oppressed all the more harshly (cf. Gen 16:6), flees from oppression, encounters God and receives His message. At the end, she shines out to be a mystique and a theologian articulating her divine experience[138] and comes back to the place of oppression but as a wife and mother and not as a slave or surrogate.[139] What Adele Berlin says of Michal and Bathsheba (in 1 Kings 1-2) as full-fledged characters will very well suit to Hagar. Regarding these two women characters, she says, "They (Michal and Bathsheba in 1 Kings 1-2) are realistically portrayed; their emotions and motivations are either made explicit or are left to be discerned by the reader from hints provided in the narrative. We feel that we know them, understand them and can, to a large extent identify with them."[140] The last statement is very much true and applicable to Hagar.

iii. Protagonists, background characters and intermediary figures

A.J. Harvey distinguishes three categories of characters: 1. protagonists 2. background characters 3. intermediary figures. We can see Hagar as protagonist. According to Tolmie protagonists, "are characterized more fully than the others, are more complex and change as the narrative progresses".[141] The explanations given above will suffice to prove that Hagar will also fit in as protagonist in Gen 16.

iv. Static and Dynamic Characters[142]

There are two kinds of characters according to Scholes and Kellogg. 1. A *static character*. It "does not evolve internally… tends to react always the same way and his or her reactions quickly become predictable".[143] It is more often 'types' which are stereotyped. 2. A *dynamic character*. It "does develop internally during the narrative".[144] The character of Hagar in Gen 16 can be called as dynamic character. Because, through the narration, she is developed as a character. She is not predictable. Her reaction towards her mistress, her flight from oppression and her bold and clear response to the messenger are unpredictable.

4. Structure of the Text

Our chapter on the implied author's textual strategy is not complete without a mention on the structure of the text. This deals of the order of events.[145]

The organization of events in a text can be analyzed in two perspective: 1. events organized syntagmatically i.e narrated one after the other. This is also called surface structure of events.

2. paradigmatic structure i.e the ways in which they are related to one another. This can be called deep structure of events.[1]

The surface structure: This can be done in three steps i.e a. paraphrasing the events b. classifying the events (such as verbal acts, non-verbal physical acts, mental acts, emotional events, sensory events etc.,) 3. determining the relationship between the events (such as hierarchy which includes kernels and satellites; micro sequences which includes time, causality, space, character and internal relationships).

The deep structure of events: We have to uncover the underlying logic of the narratives. The logical relations can be in terms of a. contradictory- mutually exclusive, b. contrary (mutually inclusive), c. complementary – absence of one is a condition for the presence of the other element.

Ska has another way of explaining the structure of the text as 'episode and scene'.[146] According to him the first subdivision of a larger narrative is an 'episode' and the subdivisions of an episode 'scenes'. A series of scenes can be called a 'sequence' or an 'act'. Keeping the above explanations as base, we can consider the Hagar story in Gen 16 as an episode, which contains acts and scenes.

Structure of Gen 16[147]

Keeping in mind how the commentators have divided Gen 16,[148] I am proposing astructure for it. This structure is devised alsowith the purpose of finding out where is the emphasis of the implied author to get the main message of the episode.Considering the change of action, characters, setting, atmosphere, narrative style, time and subject matter[149] in vv. 7 and 15 I see that Gen 16 has three acts (Act one: vv.1-6;

Act two: vv.7-14, Act three 15-16).These Acts can be further divided as scenes.

Act One (vv. 1-6)

The first Act contains an exposition (v. 1) and two scenes (vv. 2-4, 5-6).

Exposition (v.1)

The first verse functions as an exposition presenting indispensible pieces of information.[150] There are various relations and connections that exist in the episode that will lead us to divide the episode into scenes, such as cause and effect,[151] parallelism and contrast. But in our episode we see more the relation of 'action' and 'reaction' in the first act. Secondly, scenes follow also according to chronological sequence (surface structure). Accordingly, we can divide Act one into two scenes in both of them there is action and reaction and chronological sequence.

Scene one (vv.2-4)

This can be subdivided into two sections. The first section consisting of a *proposal* (v.2a) and *response* (v.2b) is followed by an *action* of Sarai (v.3), which evokes a *reaction* (in the eyes of Hagar) (v.4). The four parts make an ABCD structure of this scene.

Scene two (vv.5-6)

The above pattern is seen in this scene also. Instead of 'proposal' this time Sarai *complains* about Hagar to Abram (v.5) and Abram *responds* (v.6a). Then there is an *action* (v.6b) and *reaction* (v.6c). Therefore this scene has an A'B'C'D' structure. Putting these two scenes together we have a *parallel pattern*[152] of ABCDA'B'C'D'.[153]

Act Two (vv.7-14)

This act contains only one scene.

Scene one (vv.7-14)

The scene begins with the short narration of messenger finding Hagar at the spring (v.7), then begins the long dialog between the two (vv.8-13). The three time repeated words "and the messenger of Yahweh said to her" in vv. 9-12, serves as verbal link to see them as one group. Hagar, who spoke in v. 8 about her pitiful condition of fleeing from her mistress, speaks again in v.13. But this time she speaks of her new situation after encountering Yahweh. This reversal is because of the message communicated by messenger of Yahweh. The well that appeared in v.7 is mentioned again in v.14 forming an inclusion.

Putting these together we have the following structure of this scene.

v.7 Messenger finding Hagar at the **Well**		A
v.8 *Hagar's reply* to Messenger[154]		B
v.9. Words of Messenger -	return	X
v.10. Words of Messenger -	multitude of descendants promised	X
v.11-12. Words of Messenger -	Birth of Ishmael promised	X
v.13 *Hagar's exclaim* of her experience and new situation.		B'
v.14 **Well** is named.		A'

So we have here a concentric pattern[155] (ABXB'A') where the words of the messenger are the central focus. The three messages also have another concentric structure (axa'). While v.9 (a), and 11-12 (a') speak about concrete life situations of Hagar (that she has to return and that she is conceived; will bear a son whose name will be Ishmael), v.10 (x) speaks in abstract terms about the great multitude of offspring to Hagar. In other words, while the promises in vv. 9 and 11-12 are very particular, in v.10 it is generic, abstract and theological. Again vv 9 and 11-12 speak about oppression, affliction ((hiṭʿannî) v.9, (ʿonyēḵ)v.11) that are painful experiences of Hagar. But v.10 speaks only of positive, happy expectations that she can hope for. Therefore, we can conclude that v. 10 is the center of this scene and the episode. The themes of v.10 are very much in line with the themes of Abraham cycle (multiply (2x in 10a), multitude, offspring, not be counted,).[156] So Hagar gets more or less the same blessing as Abram in Gen 13:16.

Act three (vv. 15-16)

This act also contains only one scene.

Scene one (v. 15-16)

This speaks of the fulfillment of the promise that was given by the messenger. Here both Hagar and Abram have their respective actions, while the person of Sarai is completely sidelined. As against the scene one of Act one, where the character of Sarai is one of domination and of Abram as one of yielding and between Sarai and Hagar one of Conflict, here it is one of peaceful co-existence.

It is good to compare this with v.1 where the three characters are introduced. There in v. 1 the order of personages was Sarai, Abram and at the end Hagar. Now, it is not only reversed and Hagar comes first, added to that, Sarai is found missing and the personage of Ishmael is introduced.

The episode ends mentioning the age of Abram and the fact that Hagar had given birth Ishmael to Abram. There is also inclusion between v.1 and v. 16. While Sarai's incapacity to bear a son to Abram is indicated in v.1, the fact of Hagar giving birth Ishmael for Abram is mentioned in v.16. So there exists a formal structure in this episode.[157]

The character of Abram isalso to be seen and appreciated. While he is accused and made to act according to the proposals of Sarai, thus a helpless man, now, he gets the positive role of naming the child, which is otherwise the prerogative of matriarch in the book of Genesis (cf. Gen 4:25; 19:37, 38). His subjecthood is also asserted together with that of Hagar. Thus the structure of Gen 16 can be represented in the following way.

Act one (vv.1-6)

Exposition (v.1)

Scene One (vv.2-4)

Sarai's proposal (v.2a)	A
Abram's response (v.2b)	B
Sarai's action (v.3)	C
Hagar's reaction (v.4)	D

Scene Two (vv.5-6)

Sarai's complaint (v.5)	A'
Abram's response (v.6a)	B'
Sarai's Action (v.6b)	C'
Hagar's reaction (v.6c)	D'

Act Two (vv.7-14)

Scene One (vv.7-14)

Messenger finding Hagar at the well (v.7)		A
Hagar's reply to the messenger (v.8)		B
Words of messenger – return (v.9)	a	X
Words of messenger – multitude of descendants (v.10)	x	X
Words of messenger – birth and future of Ishmael (v.11-12)	a'	X
Hagar's exclaim (v.13)		
		B'
Well is named (v.14)		A'

Act Three (v.15-16)

Scene One (vv. 15-16)

Hagar gives birth (v.15a)

Abram gives name (v.15b)

Age of Abram (v.16).

Conclusion

This chapter studied the strategies that the implied author uses in the text to communicate the message. These strategies studied the text, looking into the details of the text. The textual strategies of the implied author discussed in this chapter are Narrator Text and Character Text, Point of View or Focalization, Characterization and Structure. Now we need to study the text as a whole. In other words, we study how as a complete whole it communicates the message.

Endnotes

[1] Cf. D.F. Tolmie, *Narratology and Biblical Narratives: A Practical Guide*, San Francisco: International Scholars Publications, 1999, 130.

[2] D.F. Tolmie, *Narratology and Biblical Narratives: A Practical Guide*, San Francisco: International Scholars Publications, 1999, 116. The author studies Jn 13:1-30 to bring out the ideological perspective. Cf. D.F. Tolmie, *Narratology and Biblical Narratives: A Practical Guide*, San Francisco: International Scholars Publications, 1999, 116-143.

[3] Cf. D.F.Tolmie,*Narratology and Biblical Narratives: A Practical Guide*, San Francisco: International Scholars Publications, 1999, 116-118.

[4] Cf. J.P.Fokkelman,*Reading Biblical Narrative: An Introductory Guide*, Louisville, Kentucky: Westminster John Knox Press 1999, 67.

[5] Cf. J.P.Fokkelman,*Reading Biblical Narrative: An Introductory Guide*, Louisville, Kentucky: Westminster John Knox Press 1999, 68.

[6] For more details cf. J.P. Fokkelman, *Reading Biblical Narrative: An Introductory Guide*, Louisville, Kentucky: Westminster John Knox Press 1999, 68-72.

[7] The translation is mine.

[8] ראה verb qal participle masculine singular construct suffix 1st person common singular or "my seeing him?" cf. Antony John Baptist, *Together as Sisters: Hagar and Dalit Women*, New Delhi: ISPCK, 2012, 80-81 for literal translation and the reasons for such translation.

[9] Adele Berlin, *Poetics and Interpretation of Biblical Narrative*, Winona Lake: Eisenbrauns, 1994, 43.

[10] Adele Berlin, *Poetics and Interpretation of Biblical Narrative*, Winona Lake: Eisenbrauns, 1994, 44. Gen 22 for example for its major part is said from the point of view of Abraham.

[11] Cf. Adele Berlin, *Poetics and Interpretation of Biblical Narrative*, Winona Lake: Eisenbrauns, 1994, 47-48 for examples and explanations from the Bible. In the book of Ruth for example though the story is told from the perspective of Naomi ("we see things through her eyes, feel things as she feels them: her bereavement and loneliness, her return to Bethlehem, her bitterness and poverty, her concern with Ruth's future security, her view of Boaz, and her restoration through the birth of her grandson." (Adele Berlin, *Poetics and Interpretation of Biblical Narrative* Winona Lake, Indiana: Eisenbrauns, 1994, 84.)), Ruth is the focus of the interest point of view.

[12] Though the interest is that of Sarai at the beginning, from v.4 it shifts to that of Hagar.

[13] Cf. Adele Berlin, *Poetics and Interpretation of Biblical Narrative*, Winona Lake: Eisenbrauns, 1994,45. See there also for examples from Bible and explanation.

[14] Ska (Cf. J. L. Ska, *"Our Fathers Have Told Us" Introduction to the Analysis of Hebrew Narratives*, (SubBib 13) Rome: PIB Press, 1990, 66.) points out to another focalization. That is called "vision from behind". Here the narrator somehow 'spies' on the characters and reveals their inner thoughts and motives.

[15] Adele Berlin, *Poetics and Interpretation of Biblical Narrative*, Winona Lake: Eisenbrauns, 1994, 55. This can be of the author, or of the narrator, or of the character/s. In the Bible it is of the narrator. The ideological view of the character/s is subordinate to that of narrator.

[16] Cf. J. L. Ska, *"Our Fathers Have Told Us" Introduction to the Analysis of Hebrew Narratives*, (SubBib 13) Rome: PIB Press, 1990, 66.

[17] Cf. D.F. Tolmie, *Narratology and Biblical narratives: A Practical Guide*, San Francisco: International Scholars Publications, 1999, 32.

[18] Cf. J. L. Ska, *"Our Fathers Have Told Us" Introduction to the Analysis of Hebrew Narratives*, (SubBib 13) Rome: PIB Press, 1990, 66.

[19] Cf. D.F. Tolmie, *Narratology and Biblical narratives: A Practical Guide*, San Francisco: International Scholars Publications, 1999, 34.

[20] Cf. Adele Berlin, *Poetics and Interpretation of Biblical Narrative*, Winona Lake: Eisenbrauns, 1994, 59-73.

[21] Adele Berlin, *Poetics and Interpretation of Biblical Narrative*, Winona Lake: Eisenbrauns, 1994, 59. See there for example and explanation from Gen 38 (Tamar story).

[22] The implied author, in v. 3, calls her as wife of Abraham, with her new social status after the legal marriage has been contracted. Cf. Antony John Baptist, *Together as Sisters: Hagar and Dalit Women*, New Delhi: ISPCK, 2012, 106-108.

[23] Many would wonder why the messenger of God also calls her as 'slave-girl of Sarai' (Gen 16:8) and Sarai as her 'mistress,' ('Gen 16:9). It is more an identification of the person. It is how society has identified them. The angel used the same categories. Themessenger adopts the view of a character. (Cf. Adele Berlin, *Poetics and Interpretation of Biblical Narrative*, Winona Lake: Eisenbrauns, 1994, 60-61).

[24] Antony John Baptist, *Together as Sisters: Hagar and Dalit Women*, New Delhi: ISPCK, 2012, 102-104.

[25]Adele Berlin, *Poetics and Interpretation of Biblical Narrative*, Winona Lake: Eisenbrauns, 1994, 61. (For example cf. 1Sam 1:13).

[26] Cf. Jud 6:22 Gideon saw that....

[27] Dennis J. McCarthy, ("The Uses of Wehinnēh in Biblical Hebrew" *Bib* 61 (1980) 330-342) gives various nuances of Wehinnēh. They are excited perception, cause, occasion, condition, concession, time, purpose, result and adversatives. We try to summarize them here and quote some examples from the Bible. The precise kind of circumstances and nuances of hinneh: 1. Excited perception: this particle introduces object clause after rā'āh and such verbs. "Sometimes there is an element of wonder or the like so great that we have to supply words in translation to get the feel of the verb" (Dennis J. McCarthy, "The Uses of Wehinnēh in Biblical Hebrew" *Bib* 61 (1980), 332.) (e.g 1Kings 10:6-7; Gen 15:17; 1Sam 30:3); 2. Cause: here hinneh parallels and continues causal kî (e.gJudg 18:9 the emphasis is not seeing but the fact that the land is good; Gen 37:29; 1Kings 2:8-9); 3. Occasion: here hinneh does not indicate just time or place or motive or cause but also opportunity, an occasion which triggers another action. Here there is the occasion for further action. (e.g. 2Sam 18:11; Judg 7:17; Gen 37:7); 4. Condition: eg Lev 13:5; Deut 13:15-17; 1Sam 9:7. 5. Concession: eg. 2Kings 7:19 (even if the Lord were to open); 6. Time: temporal use e.g Gen 24:15; 1Sam 13:10; Gen 18:10; 2Sam 18:31.; 7. Purpose: eg. 2Sam 3:12 (so that I may work with you); 15:32; 1 Kings 18:7; 2Sam 16:1; 8. Result: e.g 2Sam 19:37-38; 14:7; Gen 15:3 ("the result of the situation God has created is flatly stated to Him"); 37:7. 9. Adversatives: meaning but, rather, eg. Zeph 11:6; Is 22:12; Final caution from McCarthy, "There is really no need to force the sentence into a category and exclude everything else. Rather it is rich with meaning which overlaps categories". (Dennis J. McCarthy, "The Uses of Wehinnēh in Biblical Hebrew" *Bib* 61 (1980), 341.).

[28] Dennis J. McCarthy, "The Uses of W^e*hinnēh* in Biblical Hebrew" *Bib* 61 (1980), 331.

[29] Cf. Thomas O. Lambdin, *Introduction to Biblical Hebrew*, Harvard: Darton, Longman and Todd Ltd, 1976, no.135, for various meaning of hinneh, (as a predicator of existence; with adverbial, adjectival, or participle predicates).

[30] Dennis J. McCarthy, "The Uses of W^e*hinnēh* in Biblical Hebrew" *Bib* 61 (1980), 331.

[31] J. L. Ska, *"Our Fathers Have Told Us" Introduction to the Analysis of Hebrew Narratives*, (SubBib 13) Rome: PIB Press, 1990, 68. Also cf. Shimon Bar-Efrat, *Narrative Art in the Bible*, Dorothea Shefer-Vanson (Trans) Decatur: Almond Press 1989, 35;McCarthy, Dennis J., "The Uses of Wehinnēh in Biblical Hebrew" *Bib* 61 (1980) 330-342; T. Lambdin, *Introduction to Biblical Hebrew*, Harvard: Darton, Longman and Todd Ltd, 1976, no. 135.

[32] Cf. Adele Berlin, *Poetics and Interpretation of Biblical Narrative*, Winona Lake: Eisenbrauns, 1994, 91-94- for the various ways *hinneh* is used.

[33] Cf. Adele Berlin, *Poetics and Interpretation of Biblical Narrative* Winona Lake: Eisenbrauns, 1994, 91. See there also for other usages of *hinneh* and examples to each of them.

[34] Adele Berlin, *Poetics and Interpretation of Biblical Narrative* Winona Lake: Eisenbrauns, 1994, 91. It can be best translated as Look.

[35] Shimon Bar-Efrat, *Narrative Art in the Bible*, Dorothea Shefer-Vanson (Trans) Decatur: Almond Press 1989, 35.

[36] In which case it can be translated as 'just then' or 'no sooner' etc.,

[37] She sees Hagar only as "my maidservant" and not as a person. She does not use Hagar's proper name anywhere, not even in Gen 21. Also cf. R. Alter, *The Art of Biblical Narrative*, New York: Basic Books, 1981, 54; Meir Sternberg, *The Poetics of Biblical Narrative: Ideological Literature and the Drama of Reading*, Bloomington: Indiana University Press, 1985, 52-53,129-131, 137-138, 144, 174-175, 243, 256, 257, 398, 404; Adele Berlin, "Point of View in Biblical Narrative" *A Sense of Text: The Art of Language in the Study of Biblical Literature*, A Jewish Quarterly Review Supplement 1982 71-113; J. L. Ska, *"Our Fathers Have Told Us" Introduction to the Analysis of Hebrew Narratives*, (SubBib 13) Rome: PIB Press, 1990, 67; Antony John Baptist, *Together as Sisters: Hagar and Dalit Women*, New Delhi: ISPCK, 2012, 98-99.

[38] There is a criticism that the use of *hinneh* as point of view of the characters is more applicable when it comes after the verbs of seeing (e.g. Gen 24:63; Jud 3:4). But we can still hold them as referring to point of view of the character as in Gen 8:11; 24:30; 1Sam 4:13; 10:10; 19:16; 2Sam 15:32; 2Sam 16:1; 1Kings 18:7.

[39] On shifts of "perspectives" in theophanies cf. J. L. Ska, *"Our Fathers Have Told Us" Introduction to the Analysis of Hebrew Narratives*. (SubBib 13) Rome: PIB Press, 1990, 75-76. It is used mainly to convey the message that the narrator wants the reader to participate in the experience with the protagonist. Also cf. J.P. Fokkelman, *Reading Biblical Narrative: An*

Introductory Guide, Louisville: Westminster John Knox Press, 1999,140-143, where he considers the series of the use of *hinneh* "is a form of establishing connections, hence an invitation to the reader to work out the interrelations between these passages" (p.141).

[40] For example see 2Sam 13:8 and for the explanation cf. Adele Berlin, *Poetics and Interpretation of Biblical Narrative* Winona Lake: Eisenbrauns, 1994, 63-64. Also cf. Gen 8:11; 24:30; 1Sam 4:13; 10:10; 19:16; 2Sam 15:32; 2Sam 16:1; 1Kings 18:7.

[41] Adele Berlin, *Poetics and Interpretation of Biblical Narrative* Winona Lake: Eisenbrauns, 1994, 64. "Interior monologue" also indicates a shift in point of view.

[42] Cf. Adele Berlin, *Poetics and Interpretation of Biblical Narrative* Winona Lake: Eisenbrauns, 1994, 64; R. Alter, *The Art of Biblical Narrative*, New York: Basic Books, 1981, 77.

[43] Adele Berlin, *Poetics and Interpretation of Biblical Narrative* Winona Lake: Eisenbrauns, 1994, 73.

[44] Adele Berlin, *Poetics and Interpretation of Biblical Narrative* Winona Lake: Eisenbrauns, 1994, 50.

[45] From J. M. Lotmanas quoted by Adele Berlin, *Poetics and Interpretation of Biblical Narrative* Winona Lake: Eisenbrauns, 1994, 52.

[46] Adele Berlin, *Poetics and Interpretation of Biblical Narrative* Winona Lake: Eisenbrauns, 1994, 82.

[47] Adele Berlin, *Poetics and Interpretation of Biblical Narrative* Winona Lake: Eisenbrauns, 1994, 54.

[48] So also the point of view of the true prophets is to be taken as true.

[49] Literature on Characterization: S. Nikaido, "Hagar and Ishmael as Literary Figures: An Intertextual Study" *VT* 51 no.2 (2001)219-242; Pamela Tamarkin Reis, "Hagar Requited" *JSOT* 87 (2000) 75-109; J. Cheryl Exum, "'Mother in Israel': A Familiar Figure Reconsidered" in Letty M. Russell, (ed.) *Feminist Interpretation of the Bible*, New York: Basil Blackwell, 1985, 76-77; D.F. Tolmie, *Narratology and Biblical Narratives. A Practical Guide*, San Francisco: International Scholars Publications, 1999; J. L. Ska, *"Our Fathers Have Told Us" Introduction to the Analysis of Hebrew Narratives*, (SubBib 13) Rome: PIB Press, 1990; R. Alter, *The Art of Biblical Narrative*, New York: Basic Books, 1981, 114-130; Shimon Bar-Efrat, *Narrative Art in the Bible*, Dorothea Shefer-Vanson (Trans) Decatur: Almond Press 1989, 47-92; Meir Sternberg, *The Poetics of Biblical Narrative. Ideological Literature and the Drama of Reading*, Bloomington: Indiana University Press, 1985, 321-341;

Adele Berlin, *Poetics and Interpretation of Biblical Narrative*, Winona Lake: Eisenbrauns, 1994, 33-42.

[50] D.F. Tolmie, *Narratology and Biblical narratives: A Practical Guide*, San Francisco: International Scholars Publications, 1999, 39.

[51] M. A. Powell, *What is Narrative Criticism?* London: SPCK, 1993, 51.

[52] M. A. Powell, *What is Narrative Criticism?* London: SPCK, 1993, 52.

[53] J. L. Ska, *"Our Fathers Have Told Us" Introduction to the Analysis of Hebrew Narratives*, (SubBib 13) Rome: PIB Press, 1990, 83.

[54] Shimon Bar-Efrat, *Narrative Art in the Bible*, Dorothea Shefer-Vanson (Trans) Decatur: Almond Press 1989, 47.

[55] Adele Berlin, *Poetics and Interpretation of Biblical Narrative*, Winona Lake, Indiana: Eisenbrauns, 1994, 13.

[56] Adele Berlin, *Poetics and Interpretation of Biblical Narrative*, Winona Lake, Indiana: Eisenbrauns, 1994, 14.

[57] Shimon Bar-Efrat, *Narrative Art in the Bible*, Dorothea Shefer-Vanson (Trans) Decatur: Almond Press 1989, 90.

[58] This applies also to Hagar. The way Hagar presented in Gen 16 is different from Gen 21. In Gen 16 she is presented as an 'answering subject', while in Gen 21, she only cries out of helplessness.

[59] Shimon Bar-Efrat, *Narrative Art in the Bible*, Dorothea Shefer-Vanson (Trans) Decatur: Almond Press 1989, 91.

[60] R. Alter, *The Art of Biblical Narrative*. New York: Basic Books, 1981, 116-117 also cf. 158.

[61] M. A. Powell, *What is Narrative Criticism?* London: SPCK, 1993, 53.

[62] M. A. Powell, *What is Narrative Criticism?* London: SPCK, 1993, 53.

[63] D.F. Tolmie, *Narratology and Biblical narratives: A Practical Guide*, San Francisco: International Scholars Publications, 1999, 41.

[64] M. A. Powell, *What is Narrative Criticism?* London: SPCK, 1993, 54.

[65] Shimon Bar-Efrat, *Narrative Art in the Bible*, Dorothea Shefer-Vanson (Trans) Decatur: Almond Press 1989, 48.

[66] Shimon Bar-Efrat, *Narrative Art in the Bible*, Dorothea Shefer-Vanson (Trans) Decatur: Almond Press 1989, 48.

[67] Cf. Shimon Bar-Efrat, *Narrative Art in the Bible*, Dorothea Shefer-Vanson (Trans) Decatur: Almond Press 1989, 54.

[68] Cf. D.F. Tolmie, *Narratology and Biblical narratives: A Practical Guide*, San Francisco: International Scholars Publications, 1999, 42-43.

[69] Cf. J. L. Ska, *"Our Fathers Have Told Us" Introduction to the Analysis of Hebrew Narratives.* (SubBib 13) Rome: PIB Press, 1990, 88-89 on how the name characterizes a personage.

[70] Cf. J. L. Ska, *"Our Fathers Have Told Us" Introduction to the Analysis of Hebrew Narratives,* (SubBib 13) Rome: PIB Press, 1990,88.

[71] Shimon Bar-Efrat, *Narrative Art in the Bible,* Dorothea Shefer-Vanson (Trans) Decatur: Almond Press 1989, 84.

[72] D.F. Tolmie, *Narratology and Biblical narratives: A Practical Guide,* San Francisco: International Scholars Publications, 1999, 42.

[73] D.F. Tolmie, *Narratology and Biblical narratives: A Practical Guide,* San Francisco: International Scholars Publications, 1999, 44.

[74] Bar-Efrat however also includes minor characters (cf. Shimon Bar-Efrat, *Narrative Art in the Bible,* Dorothea Shefer-Vanson (Trans) Decatur: Almond Press 1989, 86-92).

[75] Shimon Bar-Efrat, *Narrative Art in the Bible,* Dorothea Shefer-Vanson (Trans) Decatur: Almond Press 1989, 64.

[76] Shimon Bar-Efrat, *Narrative Art in the Bible,* Dorothea Shefer-Vanson (Trans) Decatur: Almond Press 1989, 77-78.

[77] Ancient West Asian literatures speak of the conflict between maid servants and their mistress. Cf. Antony John Baptist, *Together as Sisters: Hagar and Dalit Women,* New Delhi: ISPCK, 2012, 113-114.

[78] Cf. J. L. Ska, *Abraham Cycle: Synchronic and Diachronic Analysis,* Unpublished class notes, Rome: PIB, 1996, 89.

[79] D.F. Tolmie, *Narratology and Biblical narratives: A Practical Guide,* San Francisco: International Scholars Publications, 1999, 44.

[80] Antony John Baptist, *Together as Sisters: Hagar and Dalit Women,* New Delhi: ISPCK, 2012, 115-116 and Charles Mabee, "Jacob and Laban: The Structure of Judicial Proceedings (Genesis xxxi 25-42)" *VT* 30, no. 2 (1980), 206 consider Gen 16:5 as a form of legal litigation.

[81] Literally "face"

[82] J.P. Fokkelman, *Reading Biblical Narrative: An Introductory Guide,* Louisville: Westminster John Knox Press, 1999, 144.

[83] My translation. Calling the name of Yahweh is in the sense of giving name to God, cf. Antony John Baptist, *Together as Sisters: Hagar and Dalit Women,* New Delhi: ISPCK, 2012, 151-152.

[84] Down the centuries, the patriarchal ridden society and religion manipulated, corrupted and diverted the words of Hagar. The words of

Hagar in Gen 16:13 are the most corrupt in the Hebrew original. This author had struggled to translate this verse, trying to be faithful to the text and its message. Cf.Antony John Baptist, *Together as Sisters: Hagar and Dalit Women*, New Delhi: ISPCK, 2012, 80.

[85] Originally, "the episode of Hagar may be a common popular story evolved around a god (small deity, sacred cult) called el-roi or around the sacred place called Beer-lahai-roi." 'Antony John Baptist, *Together as Sisters: Hagar and Dalit Women*, New Delhi: ISPCK, 2012, 155.' The major tradition of Yahweism would have incorporated this experience of a little tradition and identified this God "El-roi" to Yahweh (interestingly in v.13 both the names – Yahweh and El-roi - are found).

[86] J.P. Fokkelman, *Reading Biblical Narrative: An Introductory Guide*, Louisville: Westminster John Knox Press, 1999,144.

[87] Shimon Bar-Efrat, *Narrative Art in the Bible*, Dorothea Shefer-Vanson (Trans) Decatur: Almond Press 1989, 64-65.According to Berlin, "It is not only the content of the words but how they are phrased that may characterize their speaker".(Adele Berlin, *Poetics and Interpretation of Biblical Narrative*, Winona Lake: Eisenbrauns, 1994, 38.)

[88] Cf. Antony John Baptist, *Together as Sisters: Hagar and Dalit Women*, New Delhi: ISPCK, 2012, 124. When answering the messenger of God in Gen 16:8, "While the messenger was concerned about the past and the destination of Hagar, she spoke only about her present, that she is fleeing." (Antony John Baptist, *Together as Sisters: Hagar and Dalit Women*, New Delhi: ISPCK, 2012, 133-134). Also cf. Delores S. Williams, *Sisters in the Wilderness: The Challenge of Womanist God-Talk*, New York: Orbis Books, 1993, 20-21; R. D. Weis, "Stained Glass Window, Kaleidoscope or Catalyst: The Implications of Difference in Readings of the Hagar and Sarah Stories", *JSOTSS* (1996), 264; Gerald J. Janzen, "Hagar in Paul's Eyes and in the Eyes of Yahweh (Genesis 16): A Study in Horizons" *Horizons in Biblical Theology* 13 no.1 (June, 1991), 8.

[89] Cf. Shimon Bar-Efrat, *Narrative Art in the Bible*, Dorothea Shefer-Vanson (Trans) Decatur: Almond Press 1989, 66-67 on the use of polite words in Biblical narrative.

[90] Cf. Shimon Bar-Efrat, *Narrative Art in the Bible*, Dorothea Shefer-Vanson (Trans) Decatur: Almond Press 1989, 67 on absence of the polite style when the speaker's status is inferior to that of the interlocutor.

[91] Cf. Antony John Baptist, *Together as Sisters: Hagar and Dalit Women*, New Delhi: ISPCK, 2012, 127.

[92] D.F. Tolmie, *Narratology and Biblical narratives: A Practical Guide*, San Francisco: International Scholars Publications, 1999, 44. Also cf. Shimon Bar-Efrat, *Narrative Art in the Bible*, Dorothea Shefer-Vanson (Trans) Decatur: Almond Press 1989, 66.

[93] Shimon Bar-Efrat, *Narrative Art in the Bible*, Dorothea Shefer-Vanson (Trans) Decatur: Almond Press 1989, 70.

[94] Cf. D.F. Tolmie, *Narratology and Biblical narratives: A Practical Guide*, San Francisco: International Scholars Publications, 1999, 45.

[95] Cf. Num 21:17; Prov 5:15.

[96] Cf. Is 21:13-15; 8:21-22; Ps 107:4-5; Ex 15:22-25; 16:3; Ps 78:40; 95:8; Deut 8:15.

[97] Cf. Exod 19:1-2, 18, 20, 23; 24:16; 31:18; 34:29, 32; Lev 7:38; 26:46; 27:34; Neh 9:13; Num 9:5; Exod 3:1-2.

[98] J. L. Ska, *"Our Fathers Have Told Us" Introduction to the Analysis of Hebrew Narratives*, (SubBib 13) Rome: PIB Press, 1990, 88.

[99] Cf. J. L. Ska, *"Our Fathers Have Told Us" Introduction to the Analysis of Hebrew Narratives*, (SubBib 13) Rome: PIB Press, 1990, 88.

[100] Cf. J. L. Ska, *"Our Fathers Have Told Us" Introduction to the Analysis of Hebrew Narratives*, (SubBib 13) Rome: PIB Press, 1990, 89.

[101] Cf. J. L. Ska, *"Our Fathers Have Told Us" Introduction to the Analysis of Hebrew Narratives*. (SubBib 13) Rome: PIB Press, 1990, 89. For example cf. Gen 6:7; 8:21; 17:17; 18:12; 27:41; 1Sam 27:1; 1Kings 12:26-27.

[102] Cf. J. L. Ska, *"Our Fathers Have Told Us" Introduction to the Analysis of Hebrew Narratives*. (SubBib 13) Rome: PIB Press, 1990, 89-90.

[103] J. L. Ska, *"Our Fathers Have Told Us" Introduction to the Analysis of Hebrew Narratives*, (SubBib 13) Rome: PIB Press, 1990, 90.(Cf. Gen 37:15 (a man found Joseph wandering in the fields and the man asked him, "What are you seeking?"); 43:18-23).

[104] Cf. 1Sam 9:5-10 Saul and his servant looking of the donkeys.

[105] Cf. Jacob, Rachel and Leah in Gen 29:31-30:24; Manoah and his wife in Judg 13; Ahab and Jezebel in 1Kings 21.

[106] Cf. Abraham and Sarah in Gen 16 and 21.

[107] J. L. Ska, *"Our Fathers Have Told Us" Introduction to the Analysis of Hebrew Narratives*, (SubBib 13) Rome: PIB Press, 1990, 91. Though this technique is used in Gen 16:11-12, it is not used by Hagar and it does not speak of the inner feeling of Hagar either. At the most we can say

it expressed the preoccupation of Hagar, namely the safe birth of the child and its future.

[108] J. L. Ska, *"Our Fathers Have Told Us" Introduction to the Analysis of Hebrew Narratives*, (SubBib 13) Rome: PIB Press, 1990, 91. Also cf. Gen 12:1-3; 15; 16:7-12; 21:17-20; Ex 2:23-25; 3:1-4,17; 6:1, 2-8; 14:1-4, 15-18, 26.

[109] J. L. Ska, *"Our Fathers Have Told Us" Introduction to the Analysis of Hebrew Narratives*, (SubBib 13) Rome: PIB Press, 1990, 91.

[110] The other examples could be Gen 15; 19; 28:10-22; 25:22-23; Ex 3:1-4:17; 5:22-6:8; Judg 15:18-19.

[111] Cf. Shimon Bar-Efrat, *Narrative Art in the Bible*, Dorothea Shefer-Vanson (Trans) Decatur: Almond Press 1989, 86-92.

[112] Shimon Bar-Efrat, *Narrative Art in the Bible*, Dorothea Shefer-Vanson (Trans) Decatur: Almond Press 1989, 86.

[113] Cf. Shimon Bar-Efrat, *Narrative Art in the Bible*, Dorothea Shefer-Vanson (Trans) Decatur: Almond Press 1989, 87 on how the negative behavior of prophet Jonah is emphasized through the positive character of sailor.

[114] Cf. D.F. Tolmie, *Narratology and Biblical narratives: A Practical Guide*, San Francisco: International Scholars Publications, 1999, 48-50, where the author takes the model of Ruth and lists the paradigm of traits (especially in p.50).

[115] Antony John Baptist, *Together as Sisters: Hagar and Dalit Women*, New Delhi: ISPCK, 2012, 94.

[116] Cf. Antony John Baptist, *Together as Sisters: Hagar and Dalit Women*, New Delhi: ISPCK, 2012, 124. I have termed it as 'greater oppression' which is different from oppression in the normal situation. Cf. Antony John Baptist, *Together as Sisters: Hagar and Dalit Women*, New Delhi: ISPCK, 2012, 174.

[117] Cf. Antony John Baptist, *Together as Sisters: Hagar and Dalit Women*, New Delhi: ISPCK, 2012, 128-129.

[118] Cf. Antony John Baptist, *Together as Sisters: Hagar and Dalit Women*, New Delhi: ISPCK, 2012, 157-160, especially in p.157 the comparison between the first verse and the last two verses.

[119] Cf. D.F. Tolmie, *Narratology and Biblical narratives. A Practical Guide*, San Francisco: International Scholars Publications, 1999, 54- 59, 122-123; J. L. Ska, *"Our Fathers Have Told Us" Introduction to the Analysis of Hebrew Narratives*, (SubBib 13) Rome: PIB Press, 1990, 83-85.

[120] D.M. Gunn, and D.N. Fewell, *Narrative in the Hebrew Bible*, Oxford: Oxford University Press. 1993,76.

[121] D.M. Gunn, and D.N. Fewell, *Narrative in the Hebrew Bible*, Oxford: Oxford University Press. 1993,76.

[122] Gunn and Fewell rightly point out about Genesis 12-50, that although they are called to be 'patriarchal story' "many of the stories are about women, women who have their own desires, their own conflicts, their own plots if you will", D.M. Gunn, and D.N. Fewell, *Narrative in the Hebrew Bible*, Oxford: Oxford University Press. 1993,76.

[123] J. L. Ska, *"Our Fathers Have Told Us" Introduction to the Analysis of Hebrew Narratives*, (SubBib 13) Rome: PIB Press, 1990, 84.

[124] M. A. Powell, *What is Narrative Criticism?* London: SPCK, 1993, 55.

[125] D.M. Gunn, and D.N. Fewell, *Narrative in the Hebrew Bible*, Oxford: Oxford University Press. 1993, 75.

[126] J. L. Ska, *"Our Fathers Have Told Us" Introduction to the Analysis of Hebrew Narratives*, (SubBib 13) Rome: PIB Press, 1990, 84. Also cf. M. A. Powell, *What is Narrative Criticism?* London: SPCK, 1993, 55.

[127] D.M. Gunn, and D.N. Fewell, *Narrative in the Hebrew Bible*, Oxford: Oxford University Press. 1993,75.

[128] May be Hagar of Gen 21 can be seen as a flat character.

[129] D.F. Tolmie, *Narratology and Biblical narratives: A Practical Guide*, San Francisco: International Scholars Publications, 1999, 54.

[130] Adele Berlin, *Poetics and Interpretation of Biblical Narrative* Winona Lake: Eisenbrauns, 1994, 23.

[131] Cf. Adele Berlin, *Poetics and Interpretation of Biblical Narrative* Winona Lake: Eisenbrauns, 1994, 23-24; D.F. Tolmie, *Narratology and Biblical narratives: A Practical Guide*, San Francisco: International Scholars Publications, 1999, 55.

[132] Adele Berlin, *Poetics and Interpretation of Biblical Narrative*, Winona Lake: Eisenbrauns, 1994, 32.

[133] Adele Berlin, *Poetics and Interpretation of Biblical Narrative*, Winona Lake: Eisenbrauns, 1994, 24.

[134] Cf. Adele Berlin, *Poetics and Interpretation of Biblical Narrative*, Winona Lake: Eisenbrauns, 1994, 25-27. We do not know anything about the obedience of both the women, whether they obeyed the command eagerly or they could not refuse. There is very little attention is given to their emotions. Or "are left to be discerned by the reader from hints provided

in the narrative"? (Adele Berlin, *Poetics and Interpretation of Biblical Narrative* Winona Lake, Indiana: Eisenbrauns, 1994, 32.)

135 This is also called as 'Moment of Delay' or 'Retardation (final suspense)'. These items will be explained in the next chapter.

136 This is to be introduced in the next chapter.

137 This is like David and Michal in 1Sam 19:11-17. According to Adele Berlin (cf. Adele Berlin, *Poetics and Interpretation of Biblical Narrative*, Winona Lake, Indiana: Eisenbrauns, 1994, 32), though generally David is the character here Michal is the main character. The same is true of Abram and Hagar.

138 Cf. Antony John Baptist, *Together as Sisters: Hagar and Dalit Women*, New Delhi: ISPCK, 2012, 150-153.

139 Cf. Antony John Baptist, *Together as Sisters: Hagar and Dalit Women*, New Delhi: ISPCK, 2012, 158-160.

140 Adele Berlin, *Poetics and Interpretation of Biblical Narrative*, Winona Lake, Indiana: Eisenbrauns, 1994, 31-32.

141 D.F. Tolmie, *Narratology and Biblical narratives: A Practical Guide*, San Francisco: International Scholars Publications, 1999, 55.

142 As explained by J. L. Ska, *"Our Fathers Have Told Us" Introduction to the Analysis of Hebrew Narratives*, (SubBib 13) Rome: PIB Press, 1990, 83-84.

143 J. L. Ska, *"Our Fathers Have Told Us" Introduction to the Analysis of Hebrew Narratives*, (SubBib 13) Rome: PIB Press, 1990, 83.

144 J. L. Ska, *"Our Fathers Have Told Us" Introduction to the Analysis of Hebrew Narratives*, (SubBib 13) Rome: PIB Press, 1990, 83.

145 Cf. D.F. Tolmie, *Narratology and Biblical narratives. A Practical Guide*, San Francisco: International Scholars Publications, 1999, 64.

146 Cf. J. L. Ska, *"Our Fathers Have Told Us" Introduction to the Analysis of Hebrew Narratives*, (SubBib 13) Rome: PIB Press, 1990, 33.

147 Check the structure in Allen P. Ross, *Creation & Blessing: A Guide to the Study and Exposition of Genesis*, Grand Rapids: Baker Books 1988. Also cf. Bruce K. Waltke, *Genesis: A Commentary*, Grand Rapids: Zondervan 2001, 249.

148 For a discussion on the structure of Gen 16 according to the commentators as having two parts, three parts and more than three parts cf. Antony John Baptist, *Together as Sisters: Hagar and Dalit Women*, New Delhi: ISPCK, 2012,81-85.

[149] Cf. J. L. Ska, *Abraham Cycle: Synchronic and Diachronic Analysis*, Unpublished class notes, Rome: PIB, 1996, 87 and for the application of these criteria in Gen 16 cf. Antony John Baptist, *Together as Sisters: Hagar and Dalit Women*, New Delhi: ISPCK, 2012,85-87.

[150] Cf. J. L. Ska, *"Our Fathers Have Told Us" Introduction to the Analysis of Hebrew Narratives*, (SubBib 13) Rome: PIB Press, 1990,21. For detailed explanation also cf. R. Alter, *The Art of Biblical Narrative*, New York: Basic Books, 1981, 80-87; Shimon Bar-Efrat,*Narrative Art in the Bible*, Dorothea Shefer-Vanson (Trans) Decatur: Almond Press 1989, 111-112.

[151] This helps for the logical progression.

[152] That means, "elements are placed parallel to each other in the same linear order" (ABC//ABC) J.P. Fokkelman, *Reading Biblical Narrative: An Introductory Guide*, Louisville: Westminster John Knox Press 1999,116.

[153] Cf. J. Gordon Wenham, *Genesis 16-50*, Word Biblical Commentary, vol.2), Dallas: Word Books Publisher, 1994, 3-4; T.D. Alexander, "The Hagar Traditions in Genesis XVI and XXI" in J. A. Emerton (ed.), Studies in the Pentateuch, *VTS* 41 (1990), 137. For pattern of structure cf. Shimon Bar-Efrat, "Some Observations on the Analysis of Structure in Biblical Narrative" *VT* 30 no.2 (1980), 170.

[154] In this verse the emphasis is on the reply of Hagar than the question of the messenger, which is only a way to pick up conversation or everyday greeting (cf. Clause Westermann, *God's Angels Need no Wings*, David L.Scheidt (Trans) Philadelphia: Fortress Press, 1978, 86). Note the use of pronoun אָנֹכִי (ʾānōḵî) in this versewhichmeans emphasis.

[155] Cf. Shimon Bar-Efrat, "Some Observations on the Analysis of Structure in Biblical Narrative", *VT* 30 no.2 (1980), 170.

[156] Cf. Claus Westermann, *Elements of Old Testament Theology*, Dougles W. Sfott (Trans), Atlanta: John Knox Press 1978, 62. One of three connecting link in patriarch is abundance with descendants.

[157] For Formal structure cf. J. L. Ska, *"Our Fathers Have Told Us" Introduction to the Analysis of Hebrew Narratives*, (SubBib 13) Rome: PIB Press, 1990, 19-20.

CHAPTER - 5

Plot

Introduction

So far we has seen the text in depth to analyse and understand the strategies employed by the implied author to communicate message. In this chapter we try to understand how a text as whole holds together and what are the elements that are involved in making the reader to read a text further to reach its completion. It is the plot of a narration that holds it together. So let us study this in detail.

Definition

In the eyes of D. M. Gunn, D.M and D. N. Fewell, "Plot is the organizing force or principle through which narrative meaning is communicated".[1] It is nothing but the link between events.

Types of the plot

There are two types of plots. In *Unified plot*, "all the episodes are relevant to the narrative and have a bearing on the outcome of the events recounted. Every episode supposes what precedes and prepares for what follows"[2] But for *Episodic plot*, "every episode is a unit in itself and does not require the clear and complete knowledge of the former episodes to be understood"[3]. Applying these theories, according to Ska, the Abraham Cycle has a thread of the promise of a son and therefore it can be called as unified plot.[4] But at the same time, as he himself mentions, it can be also seen as episodic plot.[5] Though the story of Hagar in Gen 16 suits and situates itself very well in the Abraham Cycle,[6] thus part of unified plot, it can be also studied as episodic plot. That is, Gen 16 is a unit in itself and the character of Hagar, as central character, unifies the episode thematically.[7]

There is another way of explaining the types of plots. *Plots of resolution* are plots where the main question is "what will happen?"[8] Here time, evolution and order of events are essential and development is 'unravelling' i.e., twisted. In *Plots of revelation* however, "events and happenings are of little interest".[9] The story can be summarized in a few words. Gen 16, as most of the biblical stories, will fall under the plot of resolution.[10]

R. S. Crane explains another three kinds of plot using changes that happen in the story.[11] He speaks of *Change of knowledge*, where the reader knows at the end what was unknown at the beginning (e.g. detective stories); *Change of values* concerning the character/s or evolution of the character (e.g. Psychological novels); *Change of situation*, as it happens in adventures. Here, the question to be asked is what is the *main transformation* that occurs in the story? To arrive at an answer to this question we need to ask three other questions, namely, do we learn something that we did not know at the beginning? Does a character change from good to bad or from bad to good? Or does a situation change from good to bad or from bad to good? Applying to the Hagar episode, surely and firstly there is a change of knowledge. In the beginning the reader did not know anything about the person of Hagar, even whether such a character existed, but at the end of the story he/she knows about her character as one who revolted the system of her time and who encountered God.

Secondly, the characters do change in the story. Hagar who is introduced in a sober tone, turns out to be one who revolted oppression and towards the end emerges as a good character who met God and received the promise from God. Surprisingly, Abraham who was shown in the previous chapters as good[12] is shown in Gen 16 as bad in allowing Sarai to oppress Hagar. The opening verse of Gen 16 presents Sarai as neutral character. But as the story develops she becomes an oppressor and slowly as one side-lined by the narrator. So two characters, Abraham and Sarai, "change from good to bad,"[13] while Hagar develops from sober to good character.

Formal Structure

Before analysing various parts of the plot, we have to keep in mind that the plot of a story can be condensed in one or two words. This is called Formal structure. In the view of Ska, "It is often possible to summarize a story in a pair of words, in a simple opposition that gives the essence of the story".[14] This is an abstract model of the story and an initial way of classification. The oppositions can be "order/execution, desire/fulfilment, problem/solution, conflict/resolution of the conflict".[15]

The plot of the Hagar story, in the context of the Abraham Cycle, can be seen as plot type of problem/solution.[16] The problem is about the barrenness of Sarai, the old age of both Abram and Sarai on the one hand and the promise of God to give them child and to make them great descendants, on the other hand. How this problem is going to be solved? How God is going to fulfil his promise is the main problem of the Abraham Cycle. Gen 16 is an attempt of Sarai to get a child.[17] Gen 16, therefore is the attempted solution of Sarai.

However, when we see Gen 16 alone as an episode, 'as an unit itself', requiring no knowledge of former episodes, we can say it is more about conflict and resolution of the conflict. So some more understanding about conflict and resolution is needed. Conflict can be defined as, "a clash of actions, ideas, desires, or wills".[18] Narrative criticism is concerned "in defining such conflicts, and in determining the manner in which they are developed and resolved".[19] There are various levels of conflicts: 1. Conflicts between characters: This is expressed "in terms of inconsistent points of view or incompatible character traits".[20] For example in terms of threats that parties pose to each other. 2. Conflicts between people and their environment or with the society and their fate. 3. Conflicts of characters with themselves. Gen 16 will fall under the first type.

There is another way of finding out the Formal Structure. That is, one has to compare the initial stage of the story with the final stage.[21] When we compare v.1 and vv. 15-16 of Gen 16, we see not only the conflict and resolution but also something more. At the end of the episode we see a reversal of the initial stage. In v. 1 Sarai is wife but did not bear a child to Abram. Hagar is an Egyptian and a maidservant (foreigner and in a lower status of the society). In vv. 15-16 there is no mention of Sarai at all. Hagar is said to have given birth to a son to Abram (mentioned three times). There is no mention of her nationality or lower social status. Only her name and the fact that she is the mother are given. Therefore conflict and resolution of the conflict is the main structure.[22] of Gen 16.

Different Moments of the Plot

The various stages of the plot run like this: "the plot line ascends from a calm point of departure through the stage of involvement to the climax of conflict and tension, and from there rapidly to the finishing point and tranquillity."[23] In other words, a "typical plot begins with a rising action, reaches a climax, and ends with a falling action."[24] This is called the pyramid. Thus, the classical pattern of a plot can be listed as follows:[25] Exposition, Inciting moment, Complication, Climax, Turning point, Falling action or resolution, Last delay, Denouement (conclusion). Not that in the narrative text all these will be there as listed above. They are principle articulations or backbone of the plot. In the following section, we explain these moments and apply them to Gen 16.

Exposition

Definition

Ska defines exposition as "the presentation of *indispensable* pieces of information about the state of affairs that *precedes* the beginning of the action itself."[26] It can be also defined as "the situation existing at the beginning of the action."[27]

Content and function[28]

Exposition provides background information about the following:

a. The setting of the narrative: Exposition supplies information about the place and time of the narration. This answers to the question 'when' and 'where'. Gen 16 does not mention any of these two. So this passage has to be read as continuation of the previous episode. The place therefore is believed to be at the Oaks of Mamre (Gen 14:13) and the time is to be situated basing on Gen 16:3. Though these information are lacking, the reader does not miss the message however.

b. The main characters: Exposition also answers to the question 'who' of the episode (cf. Judg 11:1-3; 1 Sam 1:1-2; 9:1-2; 25:2-3; Job 1:1-3). The information about the characters would include "their names, traits, physical appearance, state in life and the relations obtaining among them."[29] In Gen 16:1 the three characters (Sarai, Hagar and Abram) are named and their relations among them are also made clear. While Sarai is referred as wife of Abram, Hagar is mentioned as Egyptian maidservant.[30] Sometimes few characters are introduced in the course of narration as and when they appear in the story. The messenger of Yahweh in Gen 16:7 is one such character. The reader sees him together with Hagar (v.7) and recognizes him to be God when Hagar recognizes him (v.13).

c. A key to understanding: In the exposition the narrator also mentions the contract between narrator and narratee. In other words, the essential information the reader needs to understand the narration is given.[31] There are two ways of doing it. Either the narrator can give all the needed information at the beginning of the narration as it is found in Gen 16:1 or s/he can reveal it gradually.

In the Hagar episode, it is very important to understand what is the key motif around which the whole story evolves. It is found in the fact that Sarai did not bear child for Abram. In a chiastically structured sentence this problem finds its centre place. The names of Sarai and Hagar are placed at the beginning and at the end of the verse respectively. Their social status, namely that Sarai was Abram's wife and that Hagar was an Egyptian and the slave girl of Sarai are placed at the inner side immediately after their names. The essential information to understand the whole episode, that Sarai did not bear child to Abram, is placed at the centre of the sentence. Therefore, Gen 16:1 can be represented in the following way.

And Sarai, the wife of Abram, did not give birth to him,

      A   B   X

and to her was a maidservant, an Egyptian, and her name was Hagar

      B'   A'

wəśāray ʾéšet ʾaḇrāmlōʾ

A   B

yālḏāʰlôwəlāhšiṗḥāʰmiṣrîṭûšəmāhhāḡār

X   B'   A'

d. Exposition may also convey "inner conditions"[32] such as love, fear, hate and compassion. In Gen 16 there is no any mention of inner conditions. The situation is therefore very ambiguous.

e. According to Bar-Efrat, "In some cases the facts cited in the exposition, or the way they are presented, hint at later developments in the plot".[33] This author gives the example of Gen 4 (Cain and Abel) and explains how its exposition is arranged in chiastic fashion and how this structure hints at the contrast and conflict.

This can also be said of the Hagar story. As explained above, the position of two names, Sarai (A) at the very beginning of the verse and Hagar (A') at the end of the verse hints at the probability that they are going to be the two opposing poles and that it is going to be the story of conflict between these two.[34] Their social status, namely 'wife' (B) and 'maid servant' (B') referring to Sarai and Hagar respectively, is placed in the inner side immediately after their names. This indicates that the conflict and the problem between these two will be because of the two social levels. As mentioned earlier, the key problem for the conflict between the two i.e., the barrenness of Sarai, is placed at the centre (X). Thus, this verse forms an ABXB'A' structure.[35] So the author reveals that it is a conflict story. This conflict is between the socially recognised wife and her slave/ maidservant. Bar-Efrat cautions the reader saying, "attention should be paid to the way the facts are organized within the exposition."[36] It is very much true of Gen 16:1.[37]

So the above discussion makes it clear that v.1 of Hagar episode functions as exposition introducing the characters, the relation among them and the main problem around which the episode is going to evolve. Namely, there are three characters; Sarai and Hagar stand in different social standings; one is free and the other slave or dependent; barrenness or birth of the child is going to be the point of conflict.

Place of Exposition

Most of the time exposition is found at the beginning of the narrative. But sometimes, "smaller pieces of exposition are withheld to be revealed at some appropriate moment in the midst of the tale".[38] As mentioned above, in some other cases, even the characters are introduced not at the beginning but in their proper place.[39]

Shimon Bar-Efrat, notes another thing about exposition, namely, "In most cases details concerning characters and background which appeared in the exposition at the beginning are reiterated in the body of the narrative, mentioned either by the author or one of the characters".[40] This is also seen in Gen 16, where the characters and their relation among them are *repeated* in the episode either by the narrator or the characters as it is shown below.

Sarai wife of Abram	- in v.3	by the narrator
Egyptian maidservant	- in v.3	by the narrator
Maidservant	- in v.2, v.5,	by Sarai
	- inv.6	by Abram
	- in v.8	by the messenger

This kind of repetition according to him is, "to stress some matter of importance in the story".[41] In other words, "the repetition serves to draw the reader's attention to an important point".[42] In the Hagar story, social conflict among the characters is the message that the author wants to emphasize.

Inciting moment

This can be defined as "the moment in which the conflict or the problem appears for the first time and arouses the interest of the reader".[43] Gen 16 begins with the problem of barrenness of Sarai as early as in v.1 (exposition). This, in a way, 'creates' the conflict in v.4 which persists till the end. Though the inciting moment is in v.1, the real interest is aroused in the implied reader in v.4. The reader is interested to see how Sarai is going to act in the new situation. Ska would call this as, "beginning of the complication".[44]

Complication

The term refers to "the different attempts to solve the problem or the conflict".[45] Here the question of the implied reader "what will happen?" builds up the narrative tension. We do note in Gen 16 a staircase-like construction, which builds up the tension.[46] In Gen 16 there are three attempts to solve the problem, but each of them leads to another problem or complication.

The *first attempt* is by Sarai to solve the problem of her barrenness using Hagar, the maidservant, as surrogate (vv. 2-4a). When Hagar comes to the realisation of her new status as wife and mother, Sarai becomes of little account in her eyes (v.4b). Sarai tries to solve it by taking it to Abram and complaining to him about Hagar (v.5). Abram, who is patriarch and is in a position to solve the problem, complicates it by allowing or handing over his authority over Hagar to Sarai (v.6a). This can be termed as Second attempt and Complication. Then, Sarai attempts to subdue Hagar, using hard and severe oppression (v.6b). The oppression, instead of solving the conflict, complicates the issue and Hagar flees from the house of Abram, from the presence of Sarai (vv.6c, 8). This is the Third attempt and Complication. Thus Hagar brings the story to the dead end.[47]

We can present the interplay of *attempt* to solve the problem and *the complication* that emerges out of it, in the following way.

1st attempt	—	vv. 2-4a	- Sarai attempts surrogate
1st complication	—	v.4b	- Sarai becomes of little account
2nd attempt	—	v.5	- Sarai complains to Abram
2nd complication	—	v.6a	- Abram hands over Hagar to Sarai

| 3rd attempt | – v.6b | - | Sarai oppresses Hagar |
| 3rd complication | – v.6c | - | Hagar flees. |

In all the attempts, it is Sarai who initiates the attempt, complicates and worsens the situation. So, Act I ends in a deadlock. It appears as if there is no way out and we need an external force to set things right (cf. Gen 12:17; 2Sam 11: 27- 12:1).

Climax

It is "the moment of highest tension, the appearance of a decisive element or character, the final stage of a narrative progression."[48] In other words, "climax is the highest point of progression".[49] According to this definition, the flight of Hagar (v.6) can be said to be the climax or moment of highest tension. Hagar does something, which no maidservant (slave) of her time would have even thought of or dreamt of doing. This also brings out the character of Hagar to the foreground. With this continued chain of 'action –reaction', Act I reaches its culmination, the final stage.[50]

Turning Point

According to Ska, "The turning point normally inaugurates the falling action. At this point, an element appears that will lead the movement of the narrative to its conclusion".[51] He further says, that it "… corresponds to a decisive change of direction in the dramatic action."[52] According to Bar-Efrat, "The turning point comes at the very moment that the tension reaches its height".[53] In Gen 16 the appearance of the messenger of God (v.7) can be said to be the turning point. When Sarai complicates the whole issue and brings it to a dead lock, it is the appearance of the messenger that will lead the movement to a happy end. So with the introduction of the messenger begins the falling action in the Hagar episode.[54]

Resolution

This is "the solution of the initial problem".[55] In other words "the resolution is the action that resolves the conflict or problem of the plot".[56] Chatman explains this through two Greek words *peripeteia* and *peripety*(Greek: lit. 'falling upside down' : sudden passage from one state to its opposite', 'extraordinary or unforeseen event') which means, in the plot of action (resolution), a sudden passage from one state to its opposite.[57] The other form of resolution is called *anagnorisis* (literally: recognition). It means the transition from ignorance to knowledge.[58]

There is an element of *anagnorisis* in Hagar story. That is to say, Hagar, the character, undergoes the transition from ignorance of the person with whom she was talking, to the knowledge of calling the name of God (v.13). The reader also undergoes a transition from ignorance to knowledge in respect to the identity of the messenger of Yahweh. Though it is vaguely expressed earlier (v.10), it is in v.13 the reader also comes to know the name of Yahweh who spoke to Hagar. But it cannot be considered as resolution, because it is not the initial problem. The initial problem, as explained in exposition (v.1), is the barrenness of Sarai and the method she employed and the exploitation of Hagar as an object. In v.4 the problem shifts to conflict.

The resolution in the sense of *peripeteia* or *peripety* (i.e falling upside down) can be seen in vv.15-16. When we compare the situation presented in v.1 with the situation in vv.15-16, they are not only completely different but also opposite to each other. Therefore, vv.15-16 can be considered as resolution of the Hagar episode. This is very clear in the following table.

Beginning (v.1)	end of the episode (vv.15-16)
v.1 *Sarai* is the main character	-Sarai is not at all mentioned
her social status is as wife	- Sarai's social status is not mentioned
her defect or problem is barrenness	- Hagar gave birth to a son (said 3 times)
Hagar is a minor or side character	- Hagar emerges as main character, her proper name is mentioned three times
Hagar's social status is maidservant	- *Hagar's* social status as maidservant or foreigner is not mentioned
Hagar is referred only in relation to Sarai; Her social status is a foreigner (Egyptian)	-implicitly *Hagar* is the wife of Abram.
v.2 - Sarai does not address Hagar	- Hagar is addressed by God /God's messenger
Hagar is spoken of as maidservant; Sarai or Abram never say the name of Hagar.	- the messenger uses *Hagar's* proper name.
The preoccupation of Sarai is that she may be built up	- At the end it is Hagar who is build up with a nation and a son, both with some characteristics.

Therefore vv.15-16 can be considered as resolution of the Hagar episode.

Denouement

This "is the final outcome, the final state of affairs of the dramatic action ... the final situation of the narrative".[59] There is no separate denouement in Gen 16. The above resolution (vv.15-16) can also be considered as denouement.

Moment of Delay or Retardation (final suspense)

This is the moment between resolution and the final conclusion.[60] Though v.14 may appear as a moment of delay before the conclusion, it is not within the narrative time or story. It is something away from the actual story.[61] So, there is neither moment of delay nor final conclusion in Gen 16. Therefore, vv.15-16 are also to be considered as conclusion.

What Bar-Efrat says at the end of the story of Abraham's attempt to sacrifice Isaac, is also applicable to Gen 16. He says, "Everything appears to be the same as before, but as a matter of fact a very great change has occurred, though it is an internal one".[62] At the end of Gen 16 Hagar is back in the house of Abram. But the situation is not the same as we see in v.1. In fact 'a very great change has occurred'. Hagar has met the Lord and received the promise of freedom coupled with a bright future for her and her son.

The various moments of plot in Gen 16 can be summed up as follows.

Moments of plot	Hagar episode (with verse or short words)
1. Exposition	v.1
2. Inciting moment	vv.2-4
3. Complication	vv.5-6
4. Climax	v.6c flight of Hagar

5. Turning Point	vv.7-12
6. Resolution	v.13 (*anagnorisis*); vv15-16(*peripeteia*)
7. Denouement	vv. 15-16
8. Moment of delay	——

The above structure of plot can be still summarized into three basic categories 1. Exposition: This "sets up the story world and initiates the main series of events. The situation presented in an exposition is usually characterized by incompleteness, disorder, or unfulfilled desire". 2. Conflict or complication or obstacles: this may be internal or external. In Gen 16 it is external. 3. Resolution or winding up: the end represents meaning, fulfillment, completion and closure.

Elements of Plot

Labov presents a different plot model. He sees the following elements in a plot.[63]

1. Abstract: This summarizes the whole story or tells in a nutshell what the story is about.

2. Orientation: This is where the time, place, and persons of the narrative are identified. This can be also called as the setting or background. There will also be an orientation clause, as the barrenness of Sarai.

3. Complicating Action: This is the heart of the narrative (cf. Gen 16:4). This may be marked by a. temporal indicators (specific or general), or b. circumstantial clauses.

4. Evaluation : That which indicates the point of the narrative- its *raison d'etre* – can be called the evaluation. In other words, it answers the question, why s/he is telling this story and/or

why it is worth telling. May be because it is extraordinary, amusing, unexpected, or uncommon. The various forms of evaluation stop the action and focus the reader's attention on a particular facet of it in order to bring out the point(s) of the narrative or to give the narrative its meaning and direction.

There are four elements that do this: a. intensifiers (use of repetition, quantifiers, key-words (Leitwörter)), b. comparators (introduce negatives, interrogatives, and thoughts about the future). They tell what did not or cannot happen, in order to contrast with what did or will happen (cf. Ruth 3:11), c. correlatives (double appositive or double attributive), and finally d. explications (gives the reason or motivation for certain actions and generally has the force of 'while' 'though' 'because' 'since').

5. Result or Resolution: This tells what finally happened.

6. Coda: This signals that the narrative has come to an end. It cuts off the flow of the narrative and let the audience know that the story is finished. This is done either by projecting beyond the time, or by pointing to a time known to the audience (Gen 16:16) or using 'ever after'. This in other words, to the question 'and then what happened?' it answers 'that was that' or 'Nothing, I just told you what happened'. This also situates the episode in the body of known tradition, as Gen 16:16 situates Hagar story in the Abraham Cycle and his sojourn in Canaan. This is at times also done through genealogy, at times the prologue and epilogue rolled into one. In Ruth the birth of the child and naming ends the narrative.

The above discussion can be tabled as follows for Gen 16.

Elements of Plot	Equivalent in Gen 16
1. Abstract	- conflict/ resolution of conflict
2. Orientation	- Gen 16:1[64]
3. Complicating action	- Gen 16: 2-6[65]
4. Evaluation	- this is not directly stated in Gen 16
5. Result or resolution	- Gen 16:7-15;[66]
6. Coda	- v.16.

Personages in Relation to Plot

As the story develops according to the plot, the characters in the story fall into any one of the following category.

a.   hero[67] or protagonist

b.   foils

c.   functionaries or agents

d.   crowd actors, chorus, walk-ons

It is good to know something about them.

a. Hero (heroine) or Protagonist

This person is the "most indispensable to the plot. All the attention concentrates on him because he brings forward the course of events. His actions are decisive or he is the one most affected by what happens".[68] This definition very well applies to Hagar of Gen 16. On the opposite end there is "antagonist" the main adversary of the hero. In Gen 16 Sarai can be referred as antagonist.

Fokkelman defines hero as follows, "The hero is the subject of the quest, and he proceeds along the axis of his pursuit: he is on his way to the object of value that he wants to acquire or achieve".[69] There are three conditions or requirements according to Fokkelman for a character to be considered as hero/ heroine: "Is the hero the subject of a quest? Is he/she mostly or permanently present in the text? Finally, does the hero or heroine show initiative?"[70] The Hagar episode fulfils all the three conditions to say that Hagar is the heroine. 1. She is the subject of the quest. Though Sarai begins the quest (quest for a child) it is Hagar who shifts this quest to another level (quest for her subjecthood); 2. she is the only character in Gen 16 who is present in all the Acts; 3. The reaction and the flight are the two initiatives that Hagar take in Act one. So she can be considered as heroine. Fokkelman speaks of more than one quest in 1Sam 9:1-10:16.[71] In this line one can even see three quests in Gen 16:1-6 namely, 1. Sarai trying to solve the problem of barrenness 2. Hagar's quest for subjecthood and 3. Sarai's quest to tackle the disrespect shown by Hagar (counter quest to quest no.2). While the first and the third quest fail and become less important only the quest of Hagar prevails to the end and dominates the story.

b. Foils

They "appear only to enhance the qualities of other characters".[72] There is no such case in Gen 16.

c. Functionaries or Agents

In the perception of Ska, "They are merely instruments at the service of the plot".[73] Abram in Gen 16 is an agent in the hands of Sarai in Act one because he executes what Sarai wanted and he is an agent in the hand of God in Act three, where he executes what God wanted, namely naming the child.

d. Crowds or 'Walk-ons'

In any narrative, "they are completely passive and their presence has little or no bearing on the resolution of the plot."[74] This is not found in Gen 16.

The characters other than the hero/ heroine are not neutral, either they further or obstruct the quest of the hero/ heroine.[75] In case of Gen 16 Sarai and Abram obstruct the quest and messenger of Yahweh furthers it.

Concluding Remarks

In the attempt to study the text as a whole, one principle question that is raised is that how the text holds together or is held together. It is the plot which does this function. So a study on plot was taken from different perspectives, such as, Definition, Types, Formal Structure, Different moments of the plot, Elements of plot and Personages in relation to plot.

The study of any particular text is also related to such other texts that are found in other parts of the same book or other books of the Bible. They can be studied as motifs or "type scenes" which will be explained in the next chapter of this book.

Endnotes

[1] D.M. Gunn and D.N. Fewell, *Narrative in the Hebrew Bible*, Oxford: Oxford University Press. 1993, 101. Also cf. J.P. Fokkelman, *Reading Biblical Narrative: An Introductory Guide* Louisville: Westminster John Knox Press 1999, 76, "plot is the main organizing principle of a story".

[2] J. L. Ska, *"Our Fathers Have Told Us" Introduction to the Analysis of Hebrew Narratives*, (SubBib 13) Rome: PIB Press, 1990, 18.

[3] J. L. Ska, *"Our Fathers Have Told Us" Introduction to the Analysis of Hebrew Narratives*, (SubBib 13) Rome: PIB Press, 1990, 17.

[4] Cf. J. L. Ska, *"Our Fathers Have Told Us" Introduction to the Analysis of Hebrew Narratives*. (SubBib 13) Rome: PIB Press, 1990, 18.

[5] Cf. J. L. Ska, *"Our Fathers Have Told Us" Introduction to the Analysis of Hebrew Narratives*, (SubBib 13) Rome: PIB Press, 1990, 18.

[6] Ref. Antony John Baptist, *Character of Hagar in Gen 16:1-16: A Narrative Study from the Perspective of Dalit Women*, A Thesis submitted in Partial Fulfilment of the Degree of Doctor of Philosophy (Ph.D) to Department of Christian Studies, University of Madras, Chennai, 2009, 90-95.

[7] Cf. J. L. Ska, *"Our Fathers Have Told Us" Introduction to the Analysis of Hebrew Narratives*, (SubBib 13) Rome: PIB Press, 1990, 17; Antony John Baptist, *Character of Hagar in Gen 16:1-16: A Narrative Study from the Perspective of Dalit Women*, A Thesis submitted in Partial Fulfilment of the Degree of Doctor of Philosophy (Ph.D) to Department of Christian Studies, University of Madras, Chennai, 2009, 88-90.

[8] J. L. Ska, *"Our Fathers Have Told Us" Introduction to the Analysis of Hebrew Narratives*, (SubBib 13) Rome: PIB Press, 1990, 18.

[9] J. L. Ska, *"Our Fathers Have Told Us" Introduction to the Analysis of Hebrew Narratives*, (SubBib 13) Rome: PIB Press, 1990, 18.

[10] Cf. J. L. Ska, *"Our Fathers Have Told Us" Introduction to the Analysis of Hebrew Narratives*, (SubBib 13) Rome: PIB Press, 1990, 18.

[11] Cf. J. L. Ska, *"Our Fathers Have Told Us" Introduction to the Analysis of Hebrew Narratives*, (SubBib 13) Rome: PIB Press, 1990, 19.

[12] God makes covenant with him (Gen 15); he is blessed by Melchizedek (Gen14); he rescues Lot (Gen 14); Generous to Lot (Gen 13); believed in God and was promised son and land (Gen 12).

[13] J. L. Ska, *"Our Fathers Have Told Us" Introduction to the Analysis of Hebrew Narratives*, (SubBib 13) Rome: PIB Press, 1990, 19. Sarai who was introduced as neutral character in Gen 11:29-31, gains the sympathy of the reader in Gen 12:11-20.

[14] J. L. Ska, *"Our Fathers Have Told Us" Introduction to the Analysis of Hebrew Narratives*, (SubBib 13) Rome: PIB Press, 1990, 19.

[15] J. L. Ska, *"Our Fathers Have Told Us" Introduction to the Analysis of Hebrew Narratives*, (SubBib 13) Rome: PIB Press, 1990, 20.

[16] The first act however can also be seen as action and reaction. Cf. Antony John Baptist, *Together as Sisters: Hagar and Dalit Women*, New

Delhi: ISPCK, 2012, 87-88 andabove, in chapter four, the argument for the structure of Gen 16.

[17] For the theme of 'son' in Gen 16 and Abraham Cycle cf Antony John Baptist, *Character of Hagar in Gen 16:1-16: A Narrative Study from the Perspective of Dalit Women*, A Thesis submitted in Partial Fulfilment of the Degree of Doctor of Philosophy (Ph.D) to Department of Christian Studies, University of Madras, Chennai, 2009, 92-93.

[18] M. A. Powell, *What is Narrative Criticism?*London: SPCK, 1993, 42.

[19] M. A. Powell, *What is Narrative Criticism?*London: SPCK, 1993, 42.

[20] M. A. Powell, *What is Narrative Criticism?*London: SPCK, 1993, 42.

[21] Cf. J. L. Ska, *"Our Fathers Have Told Us" Introduction to the Analysis of Hebrew Narratives*, (SubBib 13) Rome: PIB Press, 1990, 20.

[22] Cf. J. L. Ska, *"Our Fathers Have Told Us" Introduction to the Analysis of Hebrew Narratives*, (SubBib 13) Rome: PIB Press, 1990, 20. This formal structure in some times called 'theme'.

[23] Shimon Bar-Efrat, *Narrative Art in the Bible*, Dorothea Shefer-Vanson (Trans) Decatur: Almond Press 1989, 121. P.J. van Dyk, "The Function of So-Called Etiological Elements in Narratives" *ZAW* 102 (1990), 31 gives the plot of Gen 16 from barrenness of the woman to the fact that the slave will bear a son.

[24] Idea of G. Freytag quoted by J. L. Ska, *"Our Fathers Have Told Us" Introduction to the Analysis of Hebrew Narratives*, (SubBib 13) Rome: PIB Press, 1990, 20.

[25] Cf. J. L. Ska, *"Our Fathers Have Told Us" Introduction to the Analysis of Hebrew Narratives*, (SubBib 13) Rome: PIB Press, 1990, 20-21.

[26] J. L. Ska, *"Our Fathers Have Told Us". Introduction to the Analysis of Hebrew Narratives*, (SubBib 13) Rome: PIB Press, 1990, 21.

[27] Shimon Bar-Efrat, *Narrative Art in the Bible*, Dorothea Shefer-Vanson (Trans.) Decatur: Almond Press, 1989, 111.

[28] Here I try to summarize the ideas expressed in J. L. Ska, *"Our Fathers Have Told Us". Introduction to the Analysis of Hebrew Narratives*, (SubBib 13) Rome: PIB Press, 1990, 21-25 which is in fact summary of various authors. We also would refer to other authors if they differ from this or have something special to contribute.

[29] Shimon Bar-Efrat, *Narrative Art in the Bible*, Dorothea Shefer-Vanson (Trans.) Decatur: Almond Press, 1989, 111. It also provides background information and other details needed for understanding the story.

[30] Though I have translated the לה as 'she had' in fact, literally it has to be translated as "to her belongs" with a sense of possession. That is to say, Hagar is property of Sarai.

[31] Also cf. Shimon Bar-Efrat, *Narrative Art in the Bible*, Dorothea Shefer-Vanson (Trans.) Decatur: Almond Press, 1989, 111.

[32] R. Alter, *The Art of Biblical Narrative*, New York: Basic Books, 1981, 81.

[33] Shimon Bar-Efrat, *Narrative Art in the Bible*, Dorothea Shefer-Vanson (Trans.) Decatur: Almond Press, 1989, 111.

[34] Cf. Phyllis Trible, *Texts of Terror: Literary Feminist readings of Biblical Narratives*, Philadelphia: Fortress, 1984, 10.

[35] For the chiastic structure in Hebrew texts cf. above, chapter four. One, concentrating only on the names of the characters, can see Abram as centre, between the two women, and their social status. This indirectly hints at his character, as a man, who is not able to take any stand in the conflict between these two women.

[36] Shimon Bar-Efrat, *Narrative Art in the Bible*, Dorothea Shefer-Vanson (Trans.) Decatur: Almond Press, 1989, 115.

[37] The difference between the two characters is given not only because of the placing and arranging of names but because of other elements. Athalya Brenner brings out this very well. "Sarah is socially superior within the family structure and beyond it – she is a free woman who has jurisdiction over her own property and is a sole wife to her husband; Hagar is slave who is directly subordinate to Sarah, and her status vis-`a-vis Abraham is non-existent" (Athalya Brenner, "Female Social Behaviour: Two Descriptive Patterns within the "Birth of the Hero" Paradigm", *VT* 36/3 (1986) 260). The other difference concerns origin, Sarai comes originally from Abraham's immediate kin (Gen 11:26-30) and adopted sister (Gen 12; 20), but Hagar is a foreigner from Egypt. Trible brings out this contrast well by saying, "Sarai the Hebrew is married, rich, and free; she is also old and barren. Hagar the Egyptian is single, poor, and bonded; she is also young and fertile. Power belongs to Sarai, the subject of action; powerlessness marks Hagar, the object" (Phyllis Trible, *Texts of Terror: Literary Feminist readings of Biblical Narratives*, Philadelphia: Fortress, 1984, 10.). Sarai is introduced with a verb, though negative, Hagar is introduced without any verb. This goes to sharpen the difference between the two. Cf. Antony John Baptist, *Together as Sisters: Hagar and Dalit Women*, New Delhi: ISPCK, 2012, 94.

[38] R. Alter, *The Art of Biblical Narrative*, New York: Basic Books, 1981, 80-81.

[39] Cf. Shimon Bar-Efrat, *Narrative Art in the Bible*, Dorothea Shefer-Vanson (Trans.) Decatur: Almond Press, 1989, 112, 117-118.

[40] Shimon Bar-Efrat, *Narrative Art in the Bible*, Dorothea Shefer-Vanson (Trans.) Decatur: Almond Press, 1989,116.

[41] Shimon Bar-Efrat, *Narrative Art in the Bible*, Dorothea Shefer-Vanson (Trans.) Decatur: Almond Press, 1989, 116.

[42] Shimon Bar-Efrat, *Narrative Art in the Bible*, Dorothea Shefer-Vanson (Trans.) Decatur: Almond Press, 1989, 117.

[43] J. L. Ska, *"Our Fathers Have Told Us". Introduction to the Analysis of Hebrew Narratives*, (SubBib 13) Rome: PIB Press, 1990, 25.

[44] Cf. J. L. Ska, *"Our Fathers Have Told Us". Introduction to the Analysis of Hebrew Narratives*, (SubBib 13) Rome: PIB Press, 1990, 25.

[45] J. L. Ska, *"Our Fathers Have Told Us". Introduction to the Analysis of Hebrew Narratives*, (SubBib 13) Rome: PIB Press, 1990, 25.

[46] Cf. J. L. Ska, *"Our Fathers Have Told Us". Introduction to the Analysis of Hebrew Narratives*, (SubBib 13) Rome: PIB Press, 1990, 26 for biblical examples.

[47] If we observe v.4 as inciting moment, then the second and third attempts, explained above, are the complication.

[48] J. L. Ska, *"Our Fathers Have Told Us". Introduction to the Analysis of Hebrew Narratives*, (SubBib 13) Rome: PIB Press, 1990, 27.

[49] J. L. Ska, *"Our Fathers Have Told Us". Introduction to the Analysis of Hebrew Narratives*, (SubBib 13) Rome: PIB Press, 1990, 29.

[50] However vv. 11-12 can also be seen as another climax.

[51] J. L. Ska, *"Our Fathers Have Told Us". Introduction to the Analysis of Hebrew Narratives*, (SubBib 13) Rome: PIB Press, 1990, 27.

[52] J. L. Ska, *"Our Fathers Have Told Us". Introduction to the Analysis of Hebrew Narratives*, (SubBib 13) Rome: PIB Press, 1990, 29.

[53] Shimon Bar-Efrat, *Narrative Art in the Bible*, Dorothea Shefer-Vanson (Trans.) Decatur: Almond Press, 1989, 122.

[54] Cf. Gen 22: 11 (intervention of the angel of the Lord) and 2Sam 12:1 (intervention of God through Nathan).

[55] J. L. Ska, *"Our Fathers Have Told Us". Introduction to the Analysis of Hebrew Narratives*, (SubBib 13) Rome: PIB Press, 1990, 27.

[56] J. L. Ska, *"Our Fathers Have Told Us". Introduction to the Analysis of Hebrew Narratives*, (SubBib 13) Rome: PIB Press, 1990, 29.

[57] Cf. J. L. Ska, *"Our Fathers Have Told Us". Introduction to the Analysis of Hebrew Narratives*, (SubBib 13) Rome: PIB Press, 1990, 27.

[58] Cf. J. L. Ska, *"Our Fathers Have Told Us". Introduction to the Analysis of Hebrew Narratives*, (SubBib 13) Rome: PIB Press, 1990, 27.

[59] J. L. Ska, *"Our Fathers Have Told Us". Introduction to the Analysis of Hebrew Narratives*, (SubBib 13) Rome: PIB Press, 1990, 29.

[60] For examples cf. J. L. Ska, *"Our Fathers Have Told Us". Introduction to the Analysis of Hebrew Narratives*, (SubBib 13) Rome: PIB Press, 1990, 28.

[61] It can be seen as "an aetiology connecting the world of the narrative with the world of the reader, information about the origin of the story"(J. L. Ska, *"Our Fathers Have Told Us". Introduction to the Analysis of Hebrew Narratives*, (SubBib 13) Rome: PIB Press, 1990, 29). This may be a common popular story evolved around a god (small deity, sacred cult) called el-roi or around the sacred place called Beer-lahai-roi.

[62] Shimon Bar-Efrat, *Narrative Art in the Bible*, Dorothea Shefer-Vanson (Trans.) Decatur: Almond Press, 1989,122.

[63] Cf. Adele Berlin, *Poetics and Interpretation of Biblical Narrative* Winona Lake: Eisenbrauns, 1994, 102-109.

[64] Cf. Exposition above.

[65] Cf. Inciting moment, complication and climax above.

[66] Cf. Turning point and resolution above.

[67] In case of Gen 16 it is heroine

[68] J. L. Ska, *"Our Fathers Have Told Us" Introduction to the Analysis of Hebrew Narratives*, (SubBib 13) Rome: PIB Press, 1990, 86.

[69] J.P. Fokkelman, *Reading Biblical Narrative: An Introductory Guide*, Louisville: Westminster John Knox Press 1999, 78.

[70] J.P. Fokkelman, *Reading Biblical Narrative: An Introductory Guide*, Louisville: Westminster John Knox Press 1999, 82.

[71] Cf. J.P. Fokkelman, *Reading Biblical Narrative: An Introductory Guide*, Louisville: Westminster John Knox Press 1999, 87-88.

[72] J. L. Ska, *"Our Fathers Have Told Us" Introduction to the Analysis of Hebrew Narratives*, (SubBib 13) Rome: PIB Press, 1990, 87.

[73] J. L. Ska, *"Our Fathers Have Told Us" Introduction to the Analysis of Hebrew Narratives*, (SubBib 13) Rome: PIB Press, 1990, 87.

[74] J. L. Ska, *"Our Fathers Have Told Us" Introduction to the Analysis of Hebrew Narratives*, (SubBib 13) Rome: PIB Press, 1990, 87.

[75] Cf. J. P. Fokkelman, *Reading Biblical Narrative: An Introductory Guide*, Louisville, Kentucky: Westminster John Knox Press 1999, 95.

CHAPTER - 6

Type Scenes

Introduction[1]

When one reads the biblical narration s/he is sure to find lot of repetition or similarities in the way bible narrates its stories or events. There are various reasons for it, such as oral tradition, scribal error, purposeful, emphasis, and Alter particularly feels that it is because they are "compiled from parallel traditions"[2]. Though there are repetitions, there can be also small differences in the repetition. This according to Alter "could serve the purpose of commentary, analysis, foreshadowing, thematic assertion, with a wonderful combination of subtle understatement and dramatic force".[3]

Moreover, in the Biblical narrative, the episodes do not stand all alone. Especially the style of writing a particular narrative is influenced by some of the earlier writings in the Bible. There are similarities between passages that narrate similar stories in pattern and the style. They are called by different names, such as, *Leitwort*, Motif, Theme, Sequence of Actions and finally

Type Scenes. Let us try to study each of them and the Type Scenes in detail.

Alter proposes a scale of repetitive structuring and focusing devices in biblical narrative running from the smallest and most unitary elements to the largest and most composite ones.[4]

1. *Leitwort*: Alter, borrowing the words of Werker, explains it as "a word or a word-root that recurs significantly in a text, in a continuum of texts, or in a configuration of texts: by following these repetitions one is able to decipher or grasp a meaning of the text, or at any rate, the meaning will be revealed more strikingly."[5]

For example we can refer to *'go and return'* in the book of Ruth; *listen, voice* and *word* in 1Sam 15; *blessings* and *birthright* in the Jacob Cycle; *recognize, man, master, slave* and *house* in the Joseph Story; *fire* in the Samson story; *to see* in the Balam story; In Gen 16 the words referring *to see* (cf. Gen 16:4, 13),[6] *face* (cf. Gen 16:6, 8, 12),[7] *to hear* and *hand* (cf. Gen 16:6, 9, 12).[8]

2. Motif: By motif we mean that "A concrete image, sensory quality, action, or object recurs through a particular narrative."[9] In comparison to theme, this is concrete while theme implies values and therefore abstraction.

Fire in the Samson story; *stones* and the *colors white* and *red* in the Jacob story; *water* in the Moses story; *dreams, prisons* and *pits, silver* in the Joseph story, can be cited as examples. *Wilderness* (cf. Gen 16:16:7; 21:14, 20, 21), *Egypt* (cf. Gen 16:1; 21:21), and *to give birth* (cf. Gen 16:15-16) can be referred as motif in the Hagar episode.[10]

3. Theme: This can be explained as "An idea which is part of the value –system of the narrative –it may be moral, moral-

psychological, legal, political, historiosophical, theological- is made evident in some recurring pattern".[11] The theme of *affliction* (cf. Gen 16:6, 9, 11) can be the best example from Hagar story.[12]

4. Sequence of actions: This refers to Folktale form of three consecutive repetitions or three plus one, which result in a climax or a reversal. The three catastrophes, which destroyed the possessions of Job and the fourth which killed his children, can be one example.[13] In the Hagar narration there is the three time repetition of "and the messenger of Yahweh said to her" (cf. Gen 16:9, 10, 11). This can be interpreted as "there was a dialogue, discussion or argument between the messenger and Hagar."[14]

5. Type scene: This is nothing but a fixed sequence of motifs. We delve more on this topic as it is very important and widely used in the Biblical narrative.

Definitions of Type-Scene

Ska gives the definition of A. B. Lord as, "Type-scenes contain a given set of repeated elements or details, not all of which are always present, not always in the same order, but enough of which are present to make the scene a recognizable one."[15] Alter borrowing the concept of Arend defines type-scene as, "there are fixed situations which the poet is expected to include in his narrative and which he must perform according to a set of motifs."[16] Alter further defines, it as "repetitive compositional pattern."[17] Elsewhere Alter defines type – scene as, "a tacit understanding between the biblical authors and their audiences that in most cases, the portentous junctures in the life of the hero- conception and birth, initiatory trial, betrothal, deathbed- would be conveyed through a fixed sequence of narrative motifs".[18]

Some Presuppositions in Type Scenes

i.   Type Scenes do not bother or take into account matters such as, "... specific historical information- name, dates, actual practices, concrete developments".[19]

ii.   There is little possibility to find out the 'original' scene upon which others are said to be variations.

Difficulty in Type-scenes

Alter points out that, "After nearly three millennia, many of the organizing conventions of biblical narrative have been forgotten, overlaid with later logics, later ways of producing and deciphering texts, perhaps some of these conventions are now beyond recovery".[20] However, keeping this in mind, we try to explain some Biblical type-scenes.

Biblical Type-scenes

Alter[21] identifies some type-scenes in the Bible such as, annunciation, the encounter with the future betrothed at a well (Gen 24; 29:1-14; Ex 2:15-22),[22] epiphany in the field, theophany,[23] the initiatory trail,[24] danger in the desert, the discovery of a well or other source of sustenance, and the testament of the dying hero.[25] Williams[26] discusses various type-scenes that are in the Bible such as 1. the wife as sister, 2. the betrothal, 3. the agon (contest) of the barren wife 4. the promise to the barren wife. Cully[27] proposes some 'types of structures' which is equivalent to type-scenes such as A Patriarch, his wife and a Foreign Ruler (Gen 12:10-20; 20; 26:1-14), at the well (Gen 24:10-14; 29:1-14; Ex 2:15-21), visitation in the wilderness (Gen 16:6-14; 21:14-19; 1 Kings 19:4-8), a boy restored to life

(1 Kings 17:17-24; 2 Kings 4:18-37), an opportunity to kill the king (1 Sam 23:14-24:23; 26:1-25), welcome of strangers (Gen 18:1-8; 19:1-3), guests are insulted (Gen 19:4-11; Judg 19:22-25), visit of a messenger (Judg 6:11-24; 13:2-24), the prophet and the wonderful vessel (1 Kings 17:7-16; 2 Kings 4:1-7). To this long list Ska adds two more: 1. Popular Approval or installation of a ruler (Ex 14:1-31; Judg 3:7-11; 3:12-30; 6-8; 1 Sam 7:12-17; 11:1-15; 1 Kings 3:16-28); 2. Divine sanction of the Man of God (Ex 14:1-31; Num 17:16-26; Josh 3-4; 1 Sam 12:16-18; 1 Kings 18:30-39; 2 Kings 2:14-15).[28]

Let us try to explain some of them.

1. Birth of the Hero

Brenner sees the Hagar story as sample of the 'birth of the hero' myth, which can be defined as "how a hero is born despite many hardships and how he spends his early formative years".[29] The thumb rule in such narratives is that, "The more severe the circumstances described, the more impressive the results are"[30]

The short summary of this paradigm goes like this:

1. A woman is barren until quite an advanced age

2. The woman/father has revelation where the future birth and the fate of the son are announced.

3. The recipient responds. This may vary from unquestioning acceptance to incredulity.

4. The child is born.

5. The child attains maturity and fulfills his destiny despite dangers.

There are also some variations in this type-scene.

1. Two mothers with two possibilities

a. Two heroes born; one is false and one true,

b. Two mothers produce one hero

2. One mother with two possibilities

a. A single mother has two sons, or more

b. A single mother has one son

Applying these to Hagar, the two mothers in Gen 16 and 21 are different in many ways and stand opposite to each other:

Sarai: Socially superior, free woman, has jurisdiction over Hagar, her property, sole wife to her husband; immediate kin to Abraham (Gen 11:26-30), she enjoys the status of adopted sister (Gen 12 and 20); exceptionally beautiful (Gen 12:11); she enjoyed the steadfast love of Abraham; old in age; barren for long years.

Hagar: slave, subordinate to Sarah, her status is low, answerable to her mistress (v.6); foreigner from Egypt (cf. Gen 16:1); Bible is silent about her beauty; she did not enjoy anything beyond natural kindness; presumably younger; conceives shortly after she has been loaned to Abraham.[31] They are united in one purpose "to supply a son and heir to their master".[32]

According to Brenner both are to be blamed: Hagar, "For trying to use her pregnancy to ameliorate her position at the expense of her mistress"[33] (v.4) and "for attempting to run away after having been provoked"[34] and Sarai for making Hagar's life a misery and for bringing about the expulsion (Gen 21).

2. Birth Episode

There is another simple method of narrating a Birth Episode with the following elements.

1. Childlessness
2. Conception
3. Naming and reason
4. Predictions
5. Birth
6. Father's reaction.

3. Epiphany

An Epiphany episode has the following elements

1. Summoning Act
2. Saving appearance
3. Question
4. Explanation of difficulty
5. Aid

4. Annunciation Scene

According to Alter it has the following conventions:[35]

1. Plight of barrenness of the future mother

2. The distress of the barren wife is accented by the presence of a fertile, less loved co-wife.

3. The annunciation to the barren woman is enacted through the promise or prediction of an oracle, a visiting man of God, or an angel.

4. Conception and birth[36]

When Alter begins to study the various biblical passages of this type-scenes he says, "The first occurrence of the annunciation type-scene is for Sarah (Gen 18:9-15)".[37] So Alter does not see Gen 16 as the annunciation type-scene. But Raymond E. Brown[38] cites Hagar story or birth of Ishmael as first of the annunciation stories, other being Isaac (Gen 17-18), Samson (Judg 13), John the Baptist (Lk 1:11-20) and Jesus (Lk 1:26-37; Mt 1:20-21). So we can see Gen16 as annunciation type-scene.

Convention 1 : The episode (Gen 16) begins with the barrenness of the future mother (Sarai) of the hero (Isaac).

Convention 2 : There is in a way distress to the mother (Sarai) because of the fertile woman (Hagar cf. Gen 16:4-5).

Convention 3: Here there is a shift. The annunciation is not to the barren future mother but to the fertile woman/ pregnant woman/ maidservant.

Convention 4: The fertile woman/ pregnant woman/ maidservant gives birth and name is given to the child. The original mother is sidelined at least here in Gen 16.

At this juncture we have to keep in mind one thing. It is one thing to prove that a particular narrative falls under or can be grouped under a particular type-scene. But it is another and necessary thing to find out whether the author differs from the set pattern of a particular type-scene and why did s/he do so? According to Alter, "… what is really interesting is not the schema of convention but what is done in each individual application of the schema to give it a sudden tilt of innovation or even to refashion it radically for the imagination purposes at hand."[39] This way of working with the biblical text is important because, "the contemporary audience of these tales, being perfectly familiar with the convention, took particular pleasure in seeing how in each instance the convention could be, through the narrator's art, both faithfully followed and renewed for the specific needs of the hero under consideration".[40]

So we have to watch for the minute and often revelatory changes that a given type-scene undergoes as it passes from one character to another.[41] It is interesting to note that convention 1 and 2 refers to Sarai while convention 3 and 4 refers to Hagar.[42] The one who began as heroine does not remain so till the end. The one who began as villain emerges as heroine. This shift itself can be seen as revolution/ emphasis of the author/ ideology of the author. What could be the reason for this shift (from Sarai to Hagar; from the future mother to the fertile, slave woman), where the heroine (Sarai) becomes the villain and the villain (Hagar) becomes the heroine? It is v.6b, where Sarai afflicts Hagar and vv.7-12 where Hagar is in the wilderness and God meets here with a message. Therefore, basing on these verses we can infer the ideology of the implied author or his/her emphasis. Namely, God takes the side of the oppressed and subaltern.

Therefore, Gen 16 is not only revolutionary in the story line (that is, a slave girl revolting against her mistress) but it is also a revolution in the literary style of a type-scene. Firstly, it mixes two type scenes into one new type scene (i.e., agony of the barren wife and promise to the barren wife). Secondly, there is also an another revolution within this type scene. That is the one who is seen as heroine (Sarai) does not remain so till the end. The villain (Hagar) becomes the heroine at the end. And the original heroine is sidelined. In the center of all these revolutions stands the affliction of Sarai over Hagar and the pitiable plight of Hagar.[43]

In comparing other episodes of annunciation,[44] especially of Gen 25:19-25 we can make this observation. In Gen 25:21 Isaac pleads to God on behalf of his wife. But in case of Hagar nothing is mentioned about Hagar praying to God. But the messenger says, "Yahweh has listened to your affliction" (cf. Gen 16:11). May be the affliction itself is to be seen as prayer (cf. Ex 3:7,9). In comparison with Manoah who takes efforts to test the messenger to find out his identity (cf. Jud 13:8-22), Hagar, like Manoah's wife (cf. Jud 13:1-7, 23), has no difficulty in finding out the identity of the messenger as being Yahweh (cf. Gen 16:13).

4.1 Another version of annunciation

There is another version of the annunciation type scene with the following conventions.[45]

1. The *appearance* of an angel of the Lord (or appearance of the Lord) (Gen 16:7).

2. *Fear* or prostration of the visionary confronted by a supernatural presence (Gen 16:13).

3. The divine *message*:

    a. The visionary is addressed by name (Gen 16:8).

    b. A qualifying phrase describes the visionary (Gen 16:8).

    c. The visionary is urged not to be afraid.

    d. A woman is with child or is about to be with child (Gen 16:11).

    e. She will give birth to a (male) child (Gen 16:11).

    f. The name by which the child is to be called is revealed (Gen 16:11).

g. An etymology interprets the name (Gen 16:11).

h. The future accomplishments of the child are indicated (Gen 16:12).

4. An *objection* by the visionary as to how this can be, or a request for a sign.

5. The *giving* of a sign to reassure the visionary.

Comparing this outline with Gen 16 two things are missing in the Hagar episode. They also very well bring out the characteristics of Hagar 1. While other examples in the OT (Adam Gen 3:10; Abraham gen 15:1; Sarai Gen 18:15; Isaac Gen 26:24; Moses Ex 3:6) and NT (Joseph Mt 1:20; Disciple Mt 8:26; 14:27; 17:7; Mk 4:40; women Mt 28:5,10; Zacharias Lk 1:13; Mary Lk 1:30; Shepherds Lk 2:10; Simon Peter Lk 5:10) are 'afraid' and the messenger or Lord has to say not to be afraid, in the Hagar episode there is no any such discussion. So Hagar is brave without fear. 2. In the Hagar episode there is also no discussion on the sign. It is neither asked nor given. Hagar simply recognizes that the person with whom she was talking was Yahweh.

Shorter form of annunciation

The elements of annunciation according to Trible[46] are shorter. They are

1. prediction of the birth of a male child

2. the naming of the child

3. the future life of the child.

If these alone are considered then the message of the Lord to Hagar can be considered as annunciation because all these elements are found in Gen 16.

The Agon of the Barren Wife[47]

This Type scene is somewhat similar to the above but has some more details. So it is treated separately. It has the following conventions:

1. the favored wife is barren

2. there is a rival woman

3. the rival woman is fertile, bears a son for the barren woman's husband

4. the rival woman belittles the barren wife, brings about the agon (conflict, contest).

5. the barren wife is eventually heard by God, has a son.

The author, at times, goes away from these expected conventions and gives some variations. There lies the "new dramatic emphasis or a new insight"[48] of the author. In the words of Williams, "It is important, then, to note not only formal patterns but also reworking of these patterns that contribute to new plays of words, personages, images and symbols without complete departure from ancient forms".[49]

Applying the above conventions to the Hagar episode and concentrating on the deviations we find that in convention 3 the rival woman (Hagar) is only pregnant and has not yet gave birth to a child. In Convention 5, however, instead of a barren wife to be heard by God, it is the rival woman who is heard by God (cf. Gen 16:11). It is an interesting and an important twist in the story. While there are some elements of similarity there are remarkable differences too. Alter calls these variations as, "stubborn and interesting differences".[50] We also should try to find out where and why such a change is introduced. These changes and variations will point to the ideology of the implied author. This is what Alter calls as, "distinctive signals used by the ancient writers to intimate the nuanced meanings of their narratives".[51] Alter is convinced that "it is possible to get back to some of the distinctive artistic ways in which the ancient Hebrew narratives were organized".[52] Concerning Gen 16 one can say: Apart from the above mentioned variations, this story elevates a slave/ maid servant as wife (cf. Gen 16:3).

So far we have seen the various Type-Scenes in the Biblical narration and applied them to the Hagar story in Gen 16. At times we also showed how the narration of Hagar episode differs from the given type scene. But there is one event that comes very close to the Hagar story in Gen 16. That is the story of Rachel in Gen 30: 1-4. Here I would present the similarities and the difference between the two. At the end, we also will see how the narrative of Hagar episode has similarity with the non-Biblical Text. These two exercises I hope will help the reader for a better understanding of the Type scenes.

Hagar (Gen 16) and Rachel(Gen 30:1-4)[53]

These two episodes have lots of similarities. Here I give the similarities and latter present the differences.

Similarities

- "The narrator begins by reporting Rachel's perception"[54] of the situation. Sarai, in Gen 16:2, also presents her perception of the situation.[55]

- Then Rachel ends her dialogue with bitter conclusion and request (Gen 30:1). Sarai concludes her dialogue with a proposal (Gen 16:2).

- Until Gen 30, we have been told absolutely nothing of Rachel's feelings.[56] In Gen 16 we come to know something about the feelings of Sarai from her dialogue in v.2.[57] But we are not told anything about the feeling of Hagar.[58] In this way, Rachel and Hagar stand together.

- In Rachel story "Leah is not mentioned by name"[59] but instead her relationship as sister is mentioned (Gen 30:1). So also Sarai does not mention the name of Hagar in v.2.[60]

- There are lots of similarities between the arrangements made by Rachel and Sarai. Rachel says, "go in to her" (Gen 30:3) while Sarai says, "go into my maidservant" (Gen 16:2). Also the concept of being built up by the maid is reflected in both. But the idea of giving birth on one's knees (cf. Gen 30:3) is missing in Hagar episode.

- The first dialogue of Rachel shows her as "impatient, impulsive, explosive." The dialogue of Sarai also reveals the same.[61]

- What Jacob says in response to the first dialogue of Rachel namely, that God had withheld the womb of Rachel from giving birth to a child is put in the mouth of Sarai (cf. Gen 16:2).[62]

- There is a lot of similarity between what Rachel did in Gen 30:4 and what Sarai did in Gen 16:3-4. In Gen 30:4, Rachel *gave* Jacob her maid Bilhah as a wife; and Jacob went in to her and in Gen 16:3-4 Sarai ... *gave* Hagar to Abram her husband, for him as wife. And he went into Hagar. So there are similarities as the expressions of 'giving', 'as wife', 'going into' are concerned.

Differences

There are also significant differences between these two narratives. They bring out the emphasis of the implied authors of these stories.

- Gen 30:4 mentions the name of Bilhah in the first instance; then there is reference to it as personal pronoun at the end of the sentence. On the contrary, the name of Hagar is not mentioned in the first instant (cf. Gen 16:2). Instead she is mentioned by her social status, that is , as maid servant.[63] Hagar is mentioned by name only in the second instant (cf. Gen 16:8).

- While in Gen 16:2b it is said Abram listened to Sarai and did not speak anything,[64] Jacob in Gen 30 reacts rhetorically and sarcastically to the first dialogue of Rachel.[65]

- The story of Rachel is the story of barren co-wife but without annunciation. But persons such as Sarai (Gen 17-18), Hannah (1 Sam 1) and Manoah's wife (Judg 13:3-5) did receive annunciation in one way or other. In case of Hagar, she is not barren but she is a co-wife who received an annunciation.

Thus, when reading any biblical narrative the reader should look for similar incidents in the Bible either before the given passage or after. By this s/he can group the narration into a type scene and at the same time, look for the differences with other such incidents. Because it is the differences that will indicate the ideology or emphasis of the author. The differences also prove the originality and the style of the author or the implied author.

Though the Hagar story in Gen 16 has similarities with other Biblical narratives, there is hardly any narrative in the

Bible that perfectly matches the story of Gen 16. But there is a match in the Literatures of Ancient Near East. Irwin finds the following conventions.[66]

- Second wife taken because first is barren
- Birth of son to childless rich man
- Infertile Raja marries beggar woman in hope of having a son
- Jealousy of rival wives
- Persecution of pregnant co-wife
- Haughtiness of pregnant wife toward barren wife
- God as helper
- God's messenger as helper
- Rescue motif – exposed or abandoned child rescued
- Prophecy, preeminence of man's descendants
- Prophecy, unborn child to become saint
- Prophecy, unborn child to become king
- Reversal of fortune
- Success of the unpromising heroine
- Triumph of the weak.[67]

This perfectly matches with the Hagar story. So the Hagar story can be considered as a separate type scene by itself.

Endnotes

[1] Athalya Brenner, "Female Social Behaviour: Two Descriptive Patterns within the "Birth of the Hero" Paradigm" *VT* 36 no.3 (1986) 257-273.[this is on "how a hero is born despite many hardships and how he spends his early formative years" p.257.]; Dorothy Irwin, "Mytharion: the Comparison of Tales from the Old Testament and the Ancient Near East" Bergerhof, Kurt., Dietrich, Manfried., and Loretz, Oswald., (eds.)

vol. 32 *AOAT* Kevelaer: VerlagButzon & Bercker 1978. R. Alter, *The Art of Biblical Narrative*. New York: Basic Books, 1981; ———— "How Convention Helps Us Read: the Case of the Bible's Annunciation Type-Scene" *Prooftexts* 3(1983), 115-130. Edgar W. Conrad, "The Annunciation of Birth and the Birth of Messiah" *CBQ* 47 (1985), 658-659; Raymond E. Brown, *The Birth of the Messiah*, New York: Double day, 1979; Williams, James G. "The Beautiful and the Barren: Conventions in Biblical Type-Scenes" *JSOT* 17 (1980) 107-119.

[2] R. Alter, *The Art of Biblical Narrative*, New York: Basic Books, 1981, 89.

[3] R. Alter, *The Art of Biblical Narrative*, New York: Basic Books, 1981, 91.

[4] Cf. R. Alter, *The Art of Biblical Narrative*, New York: Basic Books, 1981, 88-113. There is a repetition of matters from Gen 16: 3-4 in Gen 16:5. This is seen as Sarai's interiorization of facts, as revealing the full significance of revolt of Hagar or as Sarai revealing an actual truth (cf. Antony John Baptist, *Together as Sisters: Hagar and Dalit Women*, New Delhi: ISPCK, 2012, 119-120). Here one has to take into account what Fokkelman says about repetition of words, "Even though a writer may repeat a string of words without any change, their sense and function cannot remain unaltered as the context has changed" (J.P. Fokkelman, *Reading Biblical Narrative: An Introductory Guide* Louisville: Westminster John Knox Press 1999, 121.).

[5] R. Alter, *The Art of Biblical Narrative*. New York: Basic Books, 1981, 93.

[6] Cf. Antony John Baptist, *Together as Sisters: Hagar and Dalit Women*, New Delhi: ISPCK, 2012, 153.

[7] Cf. Antony John Baptist, *Together as Sisters: Hagar and Dalit Women*, New Delhi: ISPCK, 2012, 149.

[8] Cf. Antony John Baptist, *Together as Sisters: Hagar and Dalit Women*, New Delhi: ISPCK, 2012, 150.

[9] R. Alter,*The Art of Biblical Narrative*, New York: Basic Books, 1981, 95.

[10] Cf. Antony John Baptist, *Together as Sisters: Hagar and Dalit Women*, New Delhi: ISPCK, 2012, 160.

[11] R. Alter, *The Art of Biblical Narrative*. New York: Basic Books, 1981, 95.

[12] Cf. Antony John Baptist, *Together as Sisters: Hagar and Dalit Women*, New Delhi: ISPCK, 2012, 144-145.

[13] Cf. R. Alter, *The Art of Biblical Narrative*. New York: Basic Books, 1981, 95-96.

[14] Antony John Baptist, *Together as Sisters: Hagar and Dalit Women*, New Delhi: ISPCK, 2012, 131.

[15] J. L. Ska, *"Our Fathers Have Told Us" Introduction to the Analysis of Hebrew Narratives*, (SubBib 13) Rome: PIB Press, 1990, 36.

[16] R. Alter, *The Art of Biblical Narrative*, New York: Basic Books, 1981, 50.

[17] R. Alter, *The Art of Biblical Narrative*, New York: Basic Books, 1981, 50.

[18] R. Alter, "How Convention Helps Us Read: the Case of the Bible's Annunciation Type-Scene" *Prooftexts* 3(1983), 118.

[19] James G. Williams, "The Beautiful and the Barren: Conventions in Biblical Type-Scenes" *JSOT* 17 (1980), 111.

[20] R. Alter, "How Convention Helps Us Read: the Case of the Bible's Annunciation Type-Scene" *Prooftexts* 3(1983), 116.

[21] R. Alter, *The Art of Biblical Narrative*, New York: Basic Books, 1981, 51.

[22] Cf. R. Alter, *The Art of Biblical Narrative*, New York: Basic Books, 1981, 51-62.

[23] It has the conventions such as panoramic description (Gen 16:7), internal focalization (Gen 16:13-14), external focalization (Gen 16:15-16). For more details cf. Antony John Baptist, *Together as Sisters: Hagar and Dalit Women*, New Delhi: ISPCK, 2012, 150-151.

[24] This has conventions such as Introductory Formula, Complaint Proper which includes Declaration, Accusation, Appeal for Yahweh and Judgement (Gen 16:5). For more details cf. Antony John Baptist, *Together as Sisters: Hagar and Dalit Women*, New Delhi: ISPCK, 2012, 115-116.

[25] Cf. R. Alter, *The Art of Biblical Narrative*. New York: Basic Books, 1981, 51. Gen 16 and Gen 21 can be also considered as type scenes of "bitter rivalry between a barren, favored wife and a fertile co-wife or concubine" (R. Alter, *The Art of Biblical Narrative*, New York: Basic Books, 1981, 49). It can be also considered as *annunciation* and *danger in the desert*.

[26] Cf. James G. Williams, "The Beautiful and the Barren: Conventions in Biblical Type-Scenes" *JSOT* 17 (1980) 107-119.

[27] As presented in J. L. Ska, *"Our Fathers Have Told Us" Introduction to the Analysis of Hebrew Narratives*, (SubBib 13) Rome: PIB Press, 1990, 37. He also adds examples of 'miracle stories'.

[28] Cf. J. L. Ska, *"Our Fathers Have Told Us" Introduction to the Analysis of Hebrew Narratives*, (SubBib 13) Rome: PIB Press, 1990, 38.

[29] Athalya Brenner, "Female Social Behaviour: Two Descriptive Patterns within the 'Birth of the Hero' Paradigm" *VT* 36 no.3 (1986), 257.

[30] Athalya Brenner, "Female Social Behaviour: Two Descriptive Patterns within the 'Birth of the Hero' Paradigm" *VT* 36 no.3 (1986), 257.

[31] Cf. Athalya Brenner, "Female Social Behaviour: Two Descriptive Patterns within the 'Birth of the Hero' Paradigm" *VT* 36 no.3 (1986), 260.

[32] Athalya Brenner, "Female Social Behaviour: Two Descriptive Patterns within the 'Birth of the Hero' Paradigm" *VT* 36 no.3 (1986), 261.

[33] Athalya Brenner, "Female Social Behaviour: Two Descriptive Patterns within the 'Birth of the Hero' Paradigm" *VT* 36 no.3 (1986), 261.

[34] Athalya Brenner, "Female Social Behaviour: Two Descriptive Patterns within the 'Birth of the Hero' Paradigm" *VT* 36 no.3 (1986), 261.

[35] Cf. R. Alter, "How Convention Helps Us Read: the Case of the Bible's Annunciation Type-Scene" *Prooftexts* 3(1983), 119; Antony John Baptist, *Together as Sisters: Hagar and Dalit Women*, New Delhi: ISPCK, 2012, 145.

[36] Studying the 1Sam 1 Alter sees it as the Annunciation Type-scene which has the following sections or conventions: "the barren wife's being vouchsafed an oracle, a prophecy from a man of God, or a promise from an angel, that she will be granted a son, sometimes with an explicit indication of the son's destiny" (R. Alter, *The Art of Biblical Narrative*. New York: Basic Books, 1981, 85).Also cf. Gen 18:1-15; Judg 13:2-24; 2Kings 4:8-17; Lk 1:5-25).

[37] R. Alter, "How Convention Helps Us Read: the Case of the Bible's Annunciation Type-Scene" *Prooftexts* 3(1983), 120.

[38] Raymond E. Brown, *The Birth of the Messiah: A Commentary on the Infancy Narratives in the Gospels of Mathew and Luke*, New York: Doubleday, 1993, 156.

[39] R. Alter, *The Art of Biblical Narrative*. New York: Basic Books, 1981, 52. For more examples how it is done in the biblical stories cf. R. Alter, *The Art of Biblical Narrative*. New York: Basic Books, 1981, 51-62.

[40] R. Alter, *The Art of Biblical Narrative*. New York: Basic Books, 1981, 58.

[41] Alter asks, "does the barren Rebekah's annunciation type-scene differ from Sarah's, from Hannah's, from the wife of Manoah's, from the Shunamite woman's?" (R. Alter, *The Art of Biblical Narrative*, New York: Basic Books, 1981, 181.). One also should pay attention to two type-scenes occurring in close sequence (eg. Gen 21 and Gen 22 where the younger son of Abraham is in crisis).

[42] Alter believes that the implied author gives "clues as to where the tale was going, how it differed delightfully or ingeniously or profoundly from other similar tales". (R. Alter, "How Convention Helps Us Read: the Case of the Bible's Annunciation Type-Scene" *Prooftexts* 3(1983), 128.)

[43] Cf. Antony John Baptist, *Together as Sisters: Hagar and Dalit Women*, New Delhi: ISPCK, 2012, 146.

[44] Antony John Baptist, *Together as Sisters: Hagar and Dalit Women*, New Delhi: ISPCK, 2012,146-147.

[45] Cf. Raymond E. Brown, *The Birth of the Messiah: A Commentary on the Infancy Narratives in the Gospels of Mathew and Luke*, New York: Doubleday, 1993, 156; Edgar W. Conrad, "The Annunciation of Birth and the Birth of Messiah" *CBQ* 47 (1985), 656-663. Edgar W. Conrad comments on the phrase "fear not" and says, "Brown's understanding of the structure of the "Biblical Annunciation of Birth" needs to be amended". (Edgar W. Conrad, "The Annunciation of Birth and the Birth of Messiah" *CBQ* 47 (1985), 657.) According to him Robert Neff (Robert Neff, "The Birth and Election of Isaac in the Priestly Tradition" *BR* 15 (1970) 5-18.) has argued for a fixed form in the OT concerning announcement of the birth of a son. It is contains three sections.

1. AB – "the announcement of birth introduced by the particle hinnēh"

2. N – "the designation of the name"

3. D – "the specification of the child's identity".(Edgar W. Conrad, "The Annunciation of Birth and the Birth of Messiah" *CBQ* 47 (1985), 657.) All these three elements are found in Gen 16:11-12 (Also cf. Gen 17:19; 1Kings 13:2; Isa 7:14:17; 1Chr 22:9-10).

[46] Cf. Phyllis Trible, *Texts of Terror: Literary Feminist readings of Biblical Narratives*. Philadelphia: Fortress, 1984, 16. She bases herself on the article of Robert Wilbur Neff, "The Annunciation in the Birth Narrative of Ishmael" *BiRes* 17(1972) 51-60.

[47] Cf.Gen 16:1-6; 21:1-7; 29:31-30:24; 1Sam 1.

[48] James G. Williams, "The Beautiful and the Barren: Conventions in Biblical Type-Scenes" *JSOT* 17 (1980), 111.

[49] James G. Williams, "The Beautiful and the Barren: Conventions in Biblical Type-Scenes" *JSOT* 17 (1980), 111-112. The author gives the example of annunciation to Mary in Matthew and Luke where the virginity of Mary is the variation and that is the special concern of the implied author.

[50] R. Alter, "How Convention Helps Us Read: the Case of the Bible's Annunciation Type-Scene" *Prooftexts* 3(1983), 118.

[51] R. Alter, "How Convention Helps Us Read: the Case of the Bible's Annunciation Type-Scene" *Prooftexts* 3(1983), 118.

52 R. Alter, "How Convention Helps Us Read: the Case of the Bible's Annunciation Type-Scene" *Prooftexts* 3(1983), 118.

53 Cf. R. Alter, *The Art of Biblical Narrative*. New York: Basic Books, 1981, 186-189. One can make a comparative study with other examples of the annunciation type-scenes such as Gideon (Judg 6:11-27), Samson (Judg 13), Samuel (1Sam 1), Shunamite woman (2Kings 4:8-17), Zechariah (Lk 1:5-25), and Mary (Lk 1:26-38).

54 R. Alter, *The Art of Biblical Narrative*. New York: Basic Books, 1981, 186.

55 Cf. Antony John Baptist, *Together as Sisters: Hagar and Dalit Women*, New Delhi: ISPCK, 2012,99, 101-102.

56 Cf. R. Alter, *The Art of Biblical Narrative*. New York: Basic Books, 1981,186.

57Cf. Antony John Baptist, *Together as Sisters: Hagar and Dalit Women*, New Delhi: ISPCK, 2012, 100.

58 Cf. Antony John Baptist, *Together as Sisters: Hagar and Dalit Women*, New Delhi: ISPCK, 2012, 103-104.

59 R. Alter, *The Art of Biblical Narrative*. New York: Basic Books, 1981, 186. Interestingly, in the conversation Rachel mentions the name of her maid Bilhah.

60 Cf. Antony John Baptist, *Together as Sisters: Hagar and Dalit Women*, New Delhi: ISPCK, 2012, 102-103.

61 Cf. Antony John Baptist, *Together as Sisters: Hagar and Dalit Women*, New Delhi: ISPCK, 2012, 100.

62 It is the example of women appropriating the imposed values of patriarchal system. This I term as 'internalization'. Cf. Antony John Baptist, *Together as Sisters: Hagar and Dalit Women*, New Delhi: ISPCK, 2012, 101. This has to be countered with interiorization. Cf.Antony John Baptist, *Together as Sisters: Hagar and Dalit Women*, New Delhi: ISPCK, 2012, 190-192.

63 Cf. Antony John Baptist, *Together as Sisters: Hagar and Dalit Women*, New Delhi: ISPCK, 2012, 102-103.

64 Cf. Antony John Baptist, *Together as Sisters: Hagar and Dalit Women*, New Delhi: ISPCK, 2012, 104-105.

65 Cf. R. Alter,*The Art of Biblical Narrative*. New York: Basic Books, 1981,187.